A **K.C. Flanagan, girl detective**™ adventure

Collect all the K.C. Flanagan, girl detective stories!

1. Panic in Puerto Vallarta (Oct. 1998)
2. Chaos in Cancún (Oct. 1998)
3. Mayhem in Maui (Feb. 1999)
4. Hackers from Havana (Feb. 1999)
5. Peril in Puerto Rico (May 1999)
6. Abandoned in Aruba (May 1999)

If you can't find these books at your local bookstore:

A. Complain (make it loud)
B. Place a special order
C. Order from an Internet bookstore
D. Order from the publisher (see order form at end of book)

Cataloguing in publication data

Murray, Susan, 1960-
(A K.C. Flanagan, girl detective adveture ; 1)
ISBN 1-55207-015-8

I. Davies, Robert, 1947-. II.Title. III. Series: Murray, Susan, 1960- .
K.C. Flanagan, girl detective adventure ; 1.

PZ.M972Pa 1998   j813'54   C98-941048-X

Catch all the K.C. Flanagan news on the web at
http://www.rdpppub.com/KookCase

Susan Murray and Robert Davies

PANIC IN PUERTO VALLARTA

Robert Davies Multimedia

Proofread by Alexa Leblanc, Donna Vekteris and Allyna Vineberg

Ordering information:
USA/Canada:
General Distribution Services,
1-800-387-0141/387-0172 (Canada)
1-800-805-1083(USA)
FREE FAX 1-800-481-6207
PUBNET 6307949
or from the publisher:

Robert Davies Multimedia Publishing Inc.
330-4999 St. Catherine St. West
Westmount, QC H3Z 1T3, Canada

☎ 514-481-2440
▤ 514-481-9973
e-mail: rdppub@netcom.ca

This is a work of fiction, the product of the imagination of the authors. No relation to any real people or events is intended nor should be inferred

The publisher wishes to thank the Canada Council for the Arts, the Department of Canadian Heritage, and the Sodec (Québec) for their generous support of its publishing program.

On behalf of her bird collection,
co-author Susan Murray wishes to thank
her veterinarian, Dr. Tammy Jenkins, D.V.M.
for her skill, dedication and compassion toward animals.

Co-author Robert Davies fondly remembers
a family vacation in Puerto Vallarta
with Madeleine, Alexa, Maïa and Jonah,
where K.C. was conceived, but where nothing
of any import took place except good times.

K.C.'s Introduction

"K.C.?" My father's voice echoes up the steps to my room on the third floor of our house.

"Yes?"

"We're leaving in fifteen minutes. Be there." He calls and I acknowledge his request.

"All right, Father."

Hello there. I had planned to take more time with this but I got involved in my science project and well, time really does fly. Now I have to diagram the muscles in a frog's leg and I have to finish this writing assignment since they're both due tomorrow. Also we have to go have dinner at my cousin's house tonight so I hope you forgive me if I get right to the point here.

If you're reading this then you're reading my travel diaries and I guess I should introduce myself. My name is Konstantina Cassandra Flanagan, but to my way of thinking Konstantina sounds a lot like an accordion so I prefer that my friends call me K.C. I am fourteen and three quarters years old and I live in Montreal with my older brother Rudy and my father, James Flanagan, Esq. My father is a lawyer for an international construction company based here in Montreal. He travels a lot on business and so does Linda, his Significant Other. She's a freelance photo-journalist and when she and Father travel, my brother Rudy and I often get to travel with them.

Despite the fact that they named me after Mother's weird sister and despite the fact that they're now divorced (no blame on me), my parents are pretty cool people. Father's great-grandfather came from Ireland, so he's full of blarney, something of which he misguidedly claims I have inherited. Personally I think the gift of the gab helps him in his job quite a bit.

My mother's parents are from Greece, their name is Gigantes, from an old and famous Greek Jewish family whose ancestors fought the battle of Marathon. And won! So I'm around! Mother is a sculptress and lives in both Calgary, of all places, and Dallas. She shares her life with an oil company executive named Darrell Hughes, who is actually pretty swift.

Rudy is my older brother. He's almost 18. His hobbies are sports, sports, sports and girls, girls, girls. In any order of the moment. He's actually pretty smart when he applies himself to something and like all my friends tell me, he's cute too. But don't tell him that, he already knows it! I guess he's an all right kind of brother, even if he does tease me a lot.

Anyway my point is this: I've been to a lot of really cool places and I've been keeping a diary about my travels. Some of the things that have happened to me are pretty fantastic. Rudy will tell you that I attract trouble but don't even listen to him. I mean, I guess you could say that I've been in some pretty tight spots but it's not like it's my fault. The truth is that I have a keen eye for detail and deduction. When strange things happen around me I like to investigate and find out why. I think you'll see my point when you read my story.

"K.C.?"

"Yes?"

"It's time to go, come on down."

Well, I guess that's all I have time for right now; it'll have to do. I hope you enjoy reading the story of my adventure in Mexico. It's about the lovely city of Puerto Vallarta and some mean dudes from the state of Jalisco I met there.

PANIC IN PUERTO VALLARTA

CHAPTER ONE

My brother Rudy sighed, watching as a bikini-clad tourist on a jet ski whizzed across his line of view, skipping across the waves not far from where they broke on the beach. "Man, look at that baby go."

"And the jet ski looks nice too," I commented dryly and Rudy turned a mildly affronted look on me.

"I *was* talking about the jet ski, for your information."

"Sure you were. And you hardly even noticed the girl, I bet." Rudy shrugged dismissively at my observation. As yet another scantily clad girl whizzed past us at a pretty brisk clip, his expression became that of a dog yearning for its favorite chewy toy.

"How about if we rent some jet skis too?" Rudy smiled persuasively at me but I shook my head.

"Down, boy," I replied sarcastically. He raised an eyebrow at me by way of response.

"What?" His tone was full of righteous indignation.

"You're drooling. Pull your tongue back in," I told him.

"You're just too scared," Rudy said, trying to dare me into capitulation. I shook my head to let him know it wouldn't work.

"I'm not scared. It's just that we have to meet Father in half an hour. We don't have time. Besides, you don't really want to take a ride, you just want to flirt with that girl." Another one of my cuttingly astute remarks.

Rudy ignored me and my remark, turning to watch the progress of the jet ski across the horizon of sunshine and waves, but I knew I was right. Our journey down to the waterfront had been interrupted many times as Rudy stopped every few feet to make friends.

So far the pretty juice vendor, back three blocks, and two girls selling cold bottled water had all been recipients of his smarmy smiles. Rudy is a nice guy but sometimes he gets a little carried away where members of the opposite sex are concerned. I think it's a phase he's going through.

We were standing on a stone archway overlooking a beach in the city of Puerto Vallarta, Mexico. In front of us the sand stretched gleaming, as crystal green waves frothed on the shoreline where small children ran shrieking from their approach. Now, I've traveled a lot with Father and I've certainly seen some beautiful places in my almost fifteen years, but Puerto Vallarta has to be one of the most picturesque cities I have ever visited and its waterfront is absolutely stunning.

Rudy's gaze sharpened on a solitary figure approaching us. She was tall, blond and headed toward one of the small, thatched umbrellas of woven grass dotting the beach under which tourists were seated in brightly colored chairs, sipping at exotic drinks in the shade. We watched as she sat down and began to spread suntan lotion over her bare arms and legs.

"Oh, well." Rudy shrugged and abruptly abandoned the notion of jet ski rental. "Another time I guess." He glanced down at me and I recognized the glint in his eyes. "Say, K.C., I think I'll just take a walk along the beach, check out some of the er... sights. Catch you later?" I shrugged, aware of the real reason for his sudden capitulation. My deduction was confirmed when, a moment later, he sauntered over and introduced himself to the girl under the *palapa*.

I checked my watch again. Father would be expecting

Rudy and I to join him in the lobby of the Hotel Fontana Del Mar pretty soon and Rudy was settling in, stretching himself out in the sand at his new friend's feet, charm turned fully on. I sighed, knowing from experience that it wouldn't be easy to extricate him.

"*¡Hola, Señorita!*" A voice startled me out of my reverie and I turned to find an old man behind me, beaming at me from under an enormous and colorful straw hat. He had a huge pile of handwoven blankets draped over his left shoulder and a briefcase filled with silver necklaces, rings, bracelets and earrings under his right arm. "*Señorita* like the *plata?*" he asked, doing his best to gesture at the silver he carried. I shook my head and smiled at him.

"*No, gracias.*" I rejected his offering as gently as possible. Undeterred, he pressed on.

"Blanket?" He offered, dropping the stack of them onto the handrail of the stone archway nearby. Now, I couldn't really think of any reason why I would want to buy a blanket at that particular moment. Seeing as how the sun was hot and bright overhead, the air a toasty eighty-six degrees in the shade, to my way of thinking a blanket was last on the list of things I would need.

Interpreting my hesitation as encouragement, the man grinned at me, his gold tooth gleaming fetchingly in the sun as he spread out one of the colorful handwoven blankets for my approval. And it was lovely, deep blue-green shaded into deep dusky rose with gold zig zag stripes all down the length of it.

"*Es muy bonita.*" I complimented him on its beauty.

"Fifty pesos." He nodded and smiled at my interest. "Very good price." I smiled back at him, shaking my head.

"*Gracias, no,*" I repeated and he shrugged.

"Forty-five pesos." He had lowered his voice, as though confessing a secret. "You like the blanket, no? So I give you special price." I shook my head again regretfully and he sighed then smiled and gathered up his wares. With a cheerful wave he headed off down the beach toward a middle-aged woman dozing in the sun and I watched as he stopped before her, repeating his sales pitch.

She gazed up at him groggily from behind her sunglasses, waving away the blankets but when he showed her the briefcase full of silver she sat up, and pulling her sunglasses off, leaned forward with interest. I was pleased to see him find a customer.

"K.C!" Someone called from behind me and I turned to see Father standing there. "Hey, I was just on my way to find you two. Where's Rudy?" he asked, striding across the street to join me on the bridge. I nodded toward the thatched *palapa*, under which Rudy was laughing and talking to his new friend.

"Ahh." Father nodded in comprehension and we exchanged amused glances before starting across the sand to collect my older brother. Father is about six feet tall with dark reddish brown hair and big warm brown eyes. He is one of the most good-looking people I have ever met (something which Rudy has inherited from him) and when he goes places people tend to seek him out, as though naturally drawn to his presence.

Mother tells me I resemble him but personally I think I am more a blend of both Father and Mother. I'm small, like she is, yet I have his freckles and hair, except mine is dyed dark with purple highlights. I wouldn't call myself pretty, but I think I do have an interesting face.

"How was your first day in Puerto Vallarta?" Father asked me and I grinned up at him from under my straw hat.

"Great!" I told him truthfully. "I like this town." Father smiled and tipped my hat playfully down over my eyes.

"And I like your hat," he told me, as I patiently re-adjusted it. Sometimes Father still treats me like a child but I don't hold that against him.

"I got it at that store back there." I waved toward the street behind us where a row of small market stalls spilled onto the sidewalk like a big jumble sale. Indeed, had I been so inclined I could have bought any number of things there: pens, stone carvings, masks, dolls, dresses and even shoes. "I also bought these." I paused and stretched out one foot for my father to see.

"Sandals?" He quirked an eyebrow at me and I shrugged.

"My tennis shoes were too hot," I explained. In fact, the leather sandals had been not only inexpensive but were practical as well. I hadn't expected the streets of Puerto Vallarta to be cobbled, as they were, and after watching several tourists tottering along in high heels wickedly unsuited for the situation I had resolved to buy footwear really appropriate for high-temperature walking.

"¡Hola, Rudy!" Father hailed his son as we drew near and Rudy waved back, scrambling to his feet as he introduced his new friend.

"Hey guys!" He brushed sand from his shorts and gestured at the girl beside him. "I was just coming to meet you. This is my friend, um..." A blank look crossed his face as he looked at the girl, realizing for perhaps the first time that he had yet to learn her name.

"Sandra," she told us, smiling with perfect white teeth. Her lilting accent told me that she was likely from Australia, or some place around there. "Pleased to meet you." She shifted in her chair, reaching for her drink.

"We were about to have dinner, would you care to join us?" Rudy made his move but she shook her head, waving an arm languidly at the piles of magazines she had spread on the sand around her.

"No thanks. I have tons of reading to catch up on," she replied and Rudy's face fell.

"Well, maybe I'll see you later." He smiled and left her side, looking back at her only twice as the three of us made our way back up the street toward our hotel.

The architecture of old Puerto Vallarta crowds the streets in a colorful hodgepodge of houses and shops standing shoulder to shoulder, often sharing walls. Most of the buildings we passed were commercial, consisting of little stores selling general items for tourists, but a few of them seemed to be private residences.

I glanced through the wrought iron gates of one such residence at an inner courtyard where a fountain gurgled and splashed. There was a family of Mexican people relaxing in the shade under brightly colored canopies and I smiled at the picture they made.

Next door a bored-looking girl with long, red nails sold t-shirts and film, postcards and travel maps. Rudy favored her with 'The Smile' (you know, the one he uses for first impressions) and she perked right up, leaning forward to smile back at him provocatively.

"Um," Rudy stopped in his tracks and held up a hand, glancing from Father to me, "hang on a sec guys, O.K.? I need to buy…" (here his gaze swept the girl and the rack of postcards near the counter where she stood) "…some postcards." He finished with a grin and darted into the small store.

"He doesn't waste any time, does our Rudy," Father commented thoughtfully, watching as his only son chatted up the sales girl. It was a rhetorical comment but I nodded.

"Not an instant," I said. "It *is* just a phase he's going through, right?" I added, looking at Father for confirmation of my suspicions. He shrugged and smiled a little.

"Sort of." We waited while Rudy purchased a handful of randomly selected postcards of Puerto Vallarta and rejoined us happily.

"I thought we'd eat at the Hotel Playa Los Arcos," Father informed us as we drew near the hotel. "Unless there's somewhere else you'd prefer?" Rudy and I glanced at each other then shook our heads and Father nodded briskly. "Good. They have excellent food here."

The Hotel Playa Los Arcos was four stories tall, a big white stucco building with garden balconies wrapped around it like a leafy garland. Favored by the international community, the hotel was known as much for the excellence of its accommodations as for the activities offered to its guests. Snorkeling, Spanish lessons, snacks by the pool, all these hospitalities were available, and more.

I glanced at a listing posted near the front desk for a tour to nearby Tepic, a journey which featured a volcanic *caldera*, or lake in the cone of a volcano. I'd always wanted to see one of those and made a mental note to try and talk Rudy or Father into going to Tepic with me sometime during the next week.

"Here we are." Father guided us into the lobby, through the courtyard surrounding a pool and past a veritable indoor jungle of bamboo, palm trees and a leathery red-leafed plant to a small table on an outdoor patio overlooking the beach.

A waiter in white hurried over to offer us menus and to remind us that Happy Hour was underway. I studied my menu briefly before deciding on the fresh giant shrimps, Veracruz style. Rudy took a T-bone steak, charcoal-broiled.

"I'll have the *brocheta de camarones gigantes,*" Father said with a lop-sided grin, handing the menu back to the waiter, then adding, "It's *family* dining here tonight, Gigantes kids!"

Ouch! Why do fathers make such awful puns?

"*Gracias, amigos.*" The waiter refilled our water glasses and invited us to sample the salad bar, which was served buffet style on the other side of the patio. We raised our glasses of iced tea to one other in a casual toast and then headed for the food.

"How did your day go?" Rudy asked Father as we dug in to some really attractive avocados stuffed with red pepper and bits of octopus, with *salsa mexicana* on the side.

A frown crossed Father's face. "Not as well as I'd hoped, kids," he replied, but his frown smoothed away as he took his first taste of his food. "This is really good."

"Why?" I asked him curiously.

"It's so fresh," he told me sincerely, taking another bite.

"No, not that, Dad. I meant why didn't your day go smoothly?" I clarified, and Father's frown returned.

"Well, I was given to understand that all we needed to do to conclude this real estate deal was to put the necessary paperwork in order and have all parties sign on the dotted line. As it turns out there's a bit of a problem."

"What kind of a problem?" I asked. Father shook his head, his eyes on the horizon as he replied.

"Well, the land we're interested in buying for the development is in the town of Bucerías, north of Puerto Vallarta along the coast." I nodded and he continued, "as I told you on the plane, I'm here to look the property over and check out the contract before we sign. Anyway, to make a long story short there's been a competing offer on the property."

"Another offer? You mean someone else wants to buy it too?" Father nodded and I frowned at the last shrimp on my plate. "What do they want the property for? Are they planning to develop it?" Father shrugged.

"I'm not sure. That's one of the things I'll have to find out. Tomorrow I'm planning to go have a look at the land itself, to see if we want to make a better offer on the property or whether there might be another lot in the same town which would suit our purposes just as well," here he smiled at Rudy and me, "and the two of you are more than welcome to come along if you'd like." I nodded, accepting the invitation but Rudy's eyes were fixed on something behind me.

"I don't know..." he mumbled, "I might stay here and..." I swiveled in my chair to follow the direction of his gaze across the patio to where Sandra, his erstwhile companion of the afternoon was joining her tanned and muscular boyfriend. That he was her boyfriend was obvious from the passionate kiss she bestowed on his lips. "Oh, well." Rudy's welcoming smile faded and he looked away uncomfortably, changing his plans in a flash. "Sure, why not? Bucerías sounds interesting."

"Good." Father nodded at us both. "We'll get an early start, and then have lunch there." Having worked out an acceptable plan for the following morning, we finished our meal and went back to the Hotel Fontana Del Mar where we had reservations for the duration of our stay.

The Fontana Del Mar was only a block away from the beach and it took but a minute to walk there from the Hotel Playa Los Arcos. It, too, was made of white stucco, built around an open inner courtyard, kind of like a square donut.

I marveled at the enormous fig tree growing up four floors around the stairway leading to our rooms. Hanging ferns and flowers adorned the top stories of the inner courtyard like a forest roof and bird songs echoed through the early evening air. I felt like I was in an arboretum.

To me it seemed like paradise and I was equally charmed by my room which featured huge glass doors trimmed with white wrought iron opening onto a balcony overlooking the street below. Father and Rudy took the room next door, leaving me to my own devices. I took my time unpacking my bag which we had earlier left downstairs when checking in, since our rooms had not been ready for us, and I listened to the muffled sounds of satellite sports television from the U.S. of A. coming through the wall from the men's department.

I was looking forward to a nice, relaxing vacation. It had been a particularly difficult school semester but in the end, I had managed to pull it off quite well, which is good because that's one of the conditions that Father imposes on Rudy and me. If we want to travel with him during the summer months we have to keep our grades up.

Once I was unpacked, I went out on the balcony to take some of the Puerto Vallarta evening air, and began flipping through a travel magazine when a commotion on the street below attracted my attention. I peered over the railing to where three men dressed all in white were setting up their musical instruments on the cobbled street. Clearly there was to be an impromptu performance. I saw a viola, a guitar and an accordion.

In a moment it became apparent that this was not to be the mournful serenade of romance novels; in fact it turned out to be a rollicking rendition of popular folk melodies, accompanied by much laughter and shouting back and forth between the musicians themselves.

I leaned back, relaxing again into my chair as they serenaded us and everyone else within a two block radius, minding my own business while sipping on iced water and thinking of all the fun I was going to have in Puerto Vallarta. For the whole of next week there would be nothing more complicated in my life than swimming in the warm Mexican waters and exploring this neat place.

CHAPTER TWO

Suddenly, a door slammed across the street and I looked down to see a man dressed in khaki pants and a white shirt emerge from the lobby of the hotel across the street. I watched him curiously because he glanced furtively this way then that before heading out on foot past the musicians.

I studied him closely, intrigued by his sneaky demeanor and was surprised to see him suddenly turn around and dart back towards the hotel from which he had just emerged. The reason for his abrupt change of direction became apparent as a sedan pulled up to the curb behind him and a wiry man in a dark suit emerged from the car, shouting what must have been his name.

The first man didn't respond to this hail, but instead quickened his pace. Not fast enough though, for the guy in the suit caught up to him as he was nearing the door of the hotel and roughly put a hand on his arm to detain him. They scowled at each other and I saw the man in the khakis try to pull free. The wiry man in the dark suit leaned in closer, saying something which made the first man glance around himself in panic.

The encounter between the two men was undoubtedly not one of old friends, for although they obviously knew each other there was something quite sinister about the way the guy in the suit was leaning over the first man. In fact there was something downright threatening about the way he was detaining the man in the khaki pants. My hotel travel magazine lay forgotten in my lap as I watched the scene below me unfold.

I glanced across the balcony toward Father and Rudy's room, hoping to see one or the other of them there only to find that I was alone. The musicians on the street below played on, oblivious to the drama behind them. I watched with concern as the door to the sedan opened and yet another man stepped out to join the scenario.

The second man from the car wore dark blue dress slacks with casual shoes and a polo-necked white cotton shirt with the sleeves rolled up to his elbows. I couldn't see his face at all but his build was muscular and his body seemed perfectly proportioned. When he moved he kept his head down. Together the two men escorted the man in the khakis roughly back toward the inside of the hotel.

I kept watching the entrance to the hotel across the street for several minutes, hoping to see them all emerge safely, having resolved their differences when instead, to my alarm, I heard a shout and the sound of breaking glass quite clearly even above the serenade below.

I looked up and directly across the narrow street to the balcony of the hotel opposite me. A sliding door opened and the man in khakis stumbled out, clutching at the narrow iron railing as if for support. His nose, which had been fine when I'd seen him last, was flattened and smeared with red. Blood had run down from his face onto his white shirt and he was sporting a wicked-looking bruise over his left eye.

He looked as though he had been on the receiving end of a not-so-welcoming committee. I stood up, leaning forward as though there were something I could do to help him. He glanced across at me and for a brief moment his eyes met mine. I was appalled by the look of desperation I saw there.

Then the guy in the dark suit joined him on the balcony

and punched him again, this time right in the mouth. The man in khakis toppled over sideways onto a potted palm then slid to the tiled floor of the balcony in a heap of bloodstained clothing.

Now, I guess this is where the story really begins because I found myself shouting, "Hey! Stop it!" at them, trying hard to make myself heard over the performance below. Dark Suit looked up at the sound of my voice and for a long moment we studied each other. I was particularly chilled by the flat expression on his face.

I mean, there was no anger or rage in him, none of the usual passion which accompanies an act of violence, yet I had just seen him beat someone to a pulp. He seemed oddly detached for his circumstances and I felt a flash of fear as he scowled at me then turned back to the man in khakis.

In one smooth move the man in the dark suit leaned down and hoisted his victim more or less to his feet then dragged him inside the hotel room where the other man waited, back behind the curtains. I watched, white knuckled, as Dark Suit pulled the filmy blue and white striped curtain completely closed across the balcony windows as if to block my view of what occurred next.

What he didn't take into account was the fact that the sun had set over the ocean, a glorious display of rich reds and oranges (had I been in a mood to appreciate it) and dusk was falling. Despite the drawn curtains I could see the three of them plainly silhouetted against the material and I could perfectly observe what happened.

The man in the khakis pulled drunkenly away and stood there, his shadow swaying across the light from the room and then Polo Shirt brought something heavy down on his head in a blow which was meant to crush. The man in the khakis went down and never got up again. I stood there stunned for a split second then someone turned out the lights and the room across the street was plunged into darkness.

"*Buenas noches, K.C.,*" Rudy greeted me cheerfully as he joined me on the balcony. "Man, those guys really get into their work, don't they?" I stared at him, horrified, wondering how he could be so callous, until I realized that he was referring to the musicians below us. I licked my lips. "What's the matter?" Rudy asked solicitously. "You look like you've seen a ghost." His words were lighthearted yet uncannily accurate and I nodded.

"I just saw a man killed," I told him, trying not to let my voice quaver. "I think I'd better call the police." Rudy gazed at me in astonishment.

"Killed? Where?"

"Over there." I pointed across to the balcony which was now dark and quiet. To my surprise my hand was trembling and I withdrew my pointing finger as soon as I noticed this, hoping that Rudy hadn't. "They were there, I swear it!" I insisted. Rudy stared across at the quiet balcony then back at me as he sighed.

"Now K.C. If you'll forgive my mentioning it, you do have a tendency to over-exaggerate things," he told me condescendingly. I scowled at him in protest, my alarm turning to annoyance at his refusal to believe me.

"I do not," I objected.

"You do so," he insisted mildly. I shook my head, about to explain how wrong he was but he held up a hand, assuming the Stance of The Older Brother. "What about that time in the Grand Canyon? You went and got yourself lost in the canyon all because you thought you were following an escaped prisoner. Remember?"

"But I *was* following an escaped prisoner! And because of me we caught him!" I retorted, affronted that he would dismiss my accomplishment so easily. "But that's not important right now." I turned on my heel, away from Rudy's disbelief and headed for the phone in the room. "I just saw them kill a man! I can't just sit here and do nothing." I studied the list of important numbers by the phone. Good, there it was, the number for the state police, 3 25 00.

"What's up?" Father came into my room, glancing from Rudy to where I stood clutching the phone with a frown. "Are you all right?" I shook my head.

"I just saw a man killed," I told him without preamble and Father's eyebrows shot up in surprise.

"You did? Where?" I pointed to the darkened hotel room across the street. Father quickly crossed the room to peer at it from my balcony, as I had done just minutes before.

"There's nothing there," he informed me and I shrugged impatiently.

"Well, not now there isn't, but there was. They turned out the lights right after they whacked him over the head," I said tersely, starting to dial.

"Are you absolutely sure?" Father's expression was serious, his normally good-natured smile replaced by a look of true concern. "Are you sure you didn't make a mistake? K.C., stop a minute and think." I hesitated and turned toward him, my glance falling on the street below where the musicians were packing it in for the evening.

If I hadn't been looking out at that moment I would have missed it. The man in the dark suit emerged from the hotel lobby, staggering toward the car he had left parked so haphazardly by the curb. I say 'staggered' because he and the man in dress slacks supported the limp body of the man in khakis, and it looked to me like the khaki guy was a dead weight. Literally.

Although it might have seemed to the casual observer

that the man in khakis was walking I could see that his feet simply trailed behind him on the ground. I dropped the phone and leaped across the room to the window, shouting,

"There they are!" All three men were wearing hats but I recognized their clothing. "That's them!" I shouted, leaning over the edge of the balcony.

The man in the dark suit, the one I had locked gazes with earlier, looked up and saw me staring and pointing at him. His face flushed with anger then he leaned across to speak to the man in slacks who didn't look up and they both quickened their pace, heading for the sedan.

"Someone stop them!" I shouted again, more loudly. Heads turned all up and down the street to stare at me, and the musicians all turned to look in the direction of my pointing finger. For a moment they regarded the three men passing them in utter silence then they burst into laughter. I saw one of them make a tilting motion with his hand to his mouth, as though he held a mug of beer and they all laughed again.

"K.C., calm down," Father told me gently. "It looks as though he might have had too much to drink and passed out. See? They're probably just helping him get home safely." I scowled at him and he sighed. "You must try to stop letting your imagination get the better of you." Draping a firm arm across my shoulder, Father steered me inside the room and away from the balcony. "Now let's all calm down, shall we?" I peered over my shoulder at the sedan in time to see it pull away from the curb and head down the street. It was too dark for me to make out the license plate number.

"Kook Case," Rudy muttered under his breath as he dropped into a chair by the desk in my room.

"I heard that!" I scowled blackly at him, showing my disapproval of this perversion of my nickname. "I didn't make it up. I know what I saw and I'll find a way to prove it,

Rudolph, " I insisted, deliberately using his full name. Rudy frowned and opened his mouth, no doubt to retaliate in kind.
"All right, all right. " Father held up a placating hand to prevent any further exchange of pleasantries between his beloved children. "Let's all just sit down and take it easy. I'll call down to the front desk and ask them to check on it. " After he made the call, I allowed him to provide me with a can of chilled cola from the small refrigerator in my room and sat down on the bed to sip it, studiously ignoring Rudy.

Rudy and Father are both great, I mean I wouldn't trade them for any other family in the world but sometimes they have an appalling lack of faith in me. Just because I happen to be more observant than them, and just because I like to follow up on the things I see and find out what's actually going on in the world around me they lecture me about being nosy or interfering. I've learned that at times like this it does me no good to argue and so I subsided into dignified silence, pondering what I had seen.

"K.C.'s sulking, " Rudy remarked eventually.
"I am not, " I retorted, "I'm thinking. " Father sighed and stood up as the phone rang. He picked up the receiver, and said, "Yes? Yes, no, no. Yes, I see. " Then he said to me, "K.C., they sent a man to ask outside. What you saw was just a couple of drunks on the street. Really, sweetheart, that's all it was. "

"I'm thinking I'm going to turn in, kids. Tomorrow is going to be a busy day. You two behave yourselves, all right?" with which words of adult advice he left us.

Rudy parked himself in the chair across the room, playing fast and loose with the remote control, rapidly switching channels back and forth on the television set the way he does when he's trying to annoy me, one instant on basketball, the next, on some sitcom, then back to sports. Finally I told him that I, too, was planning to get some sleep and he left.

But it wasn't until two or three in the morning that I actually did get to sleep. Every time I closed my eyes I saw the bright splash of blood on the face of the man in khakis and remembered the look on his face as he'd searched for an escape route. When I eventually dreamed, it was about being chased by sinister strangers carrying guitars which they fired at me like guns as I fled through unending darkness, unable to get away.

CHAPTER THREE

The pounding was not in my head, it was at the door of my room. I opened my eyes and blinked groggily in that direction. "K.C.! Are you in there? Wake up and open the door," Rudy's voice ordered me. I sighed and rolled out of bed, unlocking and opening the door just as he was raising a fist to pound it again.

"What?" I asked him, making no effort to keep the irritation out of my voice. In contrast to my own sleep-rumpled appearance Rudy was freshly showered, fully awake and smiling at me. He is the original revolting morning person and at the sight of him I groaned and closed my eyes.

"Ah, sleeping beauty emerges," he teased. "I like what you've done with your hair, K.C. It really does something for you." I muttered something about rude people who wake other people up for sadistic fun. "Ready for breakfast?" he continued cheerfully, although I obviously was not. "Father wants me to tell you to come downstairs, we'll be leaving for Bucerías soon. Be there or be square."

He left and I got ready in a hurry, showering and changing into lightweight white cotton pants and a long sleeved cotton blouse. I'm the type of person who sunburns easily and it was obvious that a mere application of sunblock lotion wouldn't save me from the ultra violet rays at this latitude. Anyway, I could always roll up the sleeves of my shirt if I wanted to later.

Although it was only eight in the morning, the sun was already making its presence felt. The air, thick and humid, felt sluggish, like a warm, damp cotton blanket spread over the sleeping world. But by the time I was ready to join my father and brother the slight haze which obscured the blue sky overhead had burned off. Another totally gorgeous day was under way.

The three of us crossed the street and headed for the breakfast buffet at the Hotel Playa Los Arcos. A woman washing the sidewalk in front of her shop smiled and waited until we had passed before throwing the contents of a bucket of soapy water onto the sidewalk and sweeping it clean with a rough straw broom.

Nearby was a tall brick wall surrounding an inner courtyard from which came a muted murmur of voices. When I looked inside through the gate I was surprised to see rows of students sitting in small, open classrooms as their teachers lectured them. The classrooms were separated from the sunny inner courtyard by no more than wrought iron bars. There were no panes of glass to keep the students from the warm summer air and I felt a flash of envy. It was very different from school at home in Montreal, especially in the middle of January, when I'm up to my armpits in slush and snow.

A man holding the reins of three horses in brightly studded leather saddles on the street ahead informed us that, for a few pesos, he would permit us to ride to our destination. Since we had already reached it, we smiled and shook our heads as we turned into the lobby of the Hotel Playa Los Arcos.

Breakfast was delightful, or at least it would have been if Rudy hadn't spoken up.

"See any more murders last night? he asked me through a piggish mouthful of *quesadilla* smothered in fresh *salsa*. I ignored him. "No chilling screams in the dark?" he persisted and I shot him what I hoped was a quelling look. "Did you sleep well, sweetheart?" Father asked me more politely, and I nodded.

"Sure. Fine." I wasn't about to tell either of them the truth about my nearly sleepless night and so I lapsed back into silence, concentrating on the omelette I had ordered.

"*¿Señor Flanagan?*" The waiter interrupted our meal and Father turned to him with a querying look.

"Yes?"

"Telephone call for you, very important," the waiter told him in competent English. Father gave Rudy and me a quizzical glance as he stood up and followed the waiter. He was back in two minutes with a slightly worried expression on his face.

"Listen, Rudy, K.C. I'm sorry to have to do this to you especially since I made a big deal about getting an early start," he began and Rudy and I exchanged glances, "but it looks like we're going to have to postpone our trip to Bucerías for a few hours while I attend a meeting with my clients."

I shrugged. "That's all right with me."

"No problem," Rudy agreed. Father looked relieved.

"Good. Then let's meet back at our rooms in, say, three hours. All right?" Having obtained our assent, Father left Rudy and me alone, hurrying out to the street to catch a cab at the taxi stand in front of the hotel. I finished my omelette quickly after that and stood up.

"Where are you going?" Rudy wanted to know.

"Shopping. Want to come?" I offered this blandly, secure in the knowledge that he wouldn't want to accompany me on so mundane an errand. Predictably, Rudy shook his head.

"Shopping? No thank you, ma'am."

"Fine." I squinted curiously at him. "And what are you going to do?" Rudy shrugged and shook his head.

"Oh, I don't know," he replied, his gaze riveted on one of the nearby jet ski rental docks.

"Well, drive safely," I told him, "Or should I say *jet ski* safely?" I left before he could reply.

I headed north along Olas Altas. I was glad to note that the streets were, for the most part, easy to navigate since the street names were painted in blue script on many of the stucco walls at intersections.

I was struck again by the colorful jumble of shops existing shoulder to shoulder, sharing walls yet at odds because of the nature of their wares. I saw a pizza shop next to a color copy center next to a salon right next to a law office, *Bufete de abogados* in Spanish. Sounded like lunchtime to me! There seemed to be no real order to the assemblage and this made it all the more interesting to me as I strolled along.

When I reached Ignacio Vallarta I turned left and headed north, because according to my map this would take me to the Rio Cuale, a small river which runs through the heart of the town. Sure enough, I soon found myself on a bridge wide enough for two lanes of cars, not to mention assorted foot traffic.

An old man sitting on a blanket halfway across the bridge mumbled and crooned into a makeshift karaoke machine consisting of a microphone plugged into a dusty black boombox. A battered coffee can to one side of his improvised stage contained several pesos as tourist encouragement. I liked his style and gave him all of my loose change.

After that I had to stop and look at the view from the center of the bridge. Isla Cuale below was a lush garden of palms and Indian laurel trees. The soothing gurgle of the river came to my ears along with a cool breeze which was a welcome relief in the hot sun.

Not far from where I was standing, below me on the

island itself was a stucco building painted in tasteful pastels. A neighboring billboard advertised it as the *Restaurant Cuiza* and I took the stairs down to the island and towards it, enjoying my transition to the coolness of the shade under the trees.

I reached the ground, admired the restaurant and made a mental note to ask Father to take us there for dinner some night. I was turning to go when the man in the dark suit from the night before emerged from the restaurant door and stood there for a moment, fishing in his breast pocket for a pair of sunglasses. This time he was wearing beige, but it was still definitely him.

After I realized that he hadn't seen me I ducked out of sight behind an Indian laurel tree and watched as he hurried up the stairs to the bridge. Now, I know that it might not have been the wisest thing for me to follow a known killer, but sometimes I do not choose the wise course and yes, I followed him.

He hurried along the bridge over the *Rio Cuale,* impatiently brushing past the old man with the boombox then striding along a street I identified as *Insurgentes*. It seemed logical to assume that he either lived nearby or worked somewhere in the area and I found myself wondering just where he might be going.

There are few traffic signals in that part of Puerto Vallarta. The man stood at the curbside of a busy intersection, waiting until there was a break in traffic while I loitered half a block behind him, acting as nonchalant as possible.

I followed him on into the next block where, halfway down the street, he ducked left and went down a shallow flight of steps to enter an office of some kind. Several doors away I sat down on a stool under the red and white striped beach umbrella of a street vendor and ordered a small glass of mango juice.

The office into which my quarry had fled featured a large billboard with the word *abogados* on it and it listed the type of law those particular *abogados* practiced, as well as their names. Sanchez and Sanchez were lawyers who practiced not only civil but *penal, fiscal, mercantil, laboral* and real estate law. I sipped at my juice as I read these words, acknowledging to myself that things had just become a lot more interesting.

The man in the suit stayed inside for twelve minutes, I happen to know, because I timed him using an actual timer (just one of the handy built-in features of my wristwatch). It took me a minute to come up with a plan but when I did I crossed the street to a vendor selling hand-worked leather items and quickly bought a slim black leather wallet.

The lady there charged me sixty pesos for the wallet. I knew I'd seen it for forty elsewhere but that didn't matter now because time was of the essence, so I bought it without haggling. After tucking a ten peso note inside the wallet I returned to the juice stall and this time had a glass of pineapple juice while I waited.

Like I said, it was twelve full minutes before the man came back out onto the street and when he did, he hailed a taxi in front of the office. It stopped and he got in, then it disappeared rapidly into the distance. It would have done me no good at all to take the taxi's license plate number, so I didn't even bother. Nor did I try to hail a taxi in which to follow him. I had a much better plan.

As soon as the taxi was completely out of sight, I went down the steps myself and entered the office, pretending to be somewhat winded as though from running when I addressed the young female receptionist sitting there.

"A…a man…wearing a beige suit and about this tall…" I gestured in the air over my shoulder, wiping conspicuously at my forehead. "He just left this office — what's his name?" She stared at me blankly as I continued, "He dropped this." I held out the wallet and her eyes widened in question. *"¿Señor Rodriguez?"* "The one who just left here? Wearing a beige suit?" I asked, and she nodded so I continued, improvising freely. "He hailed a taxi and left so quickly I couldn't give it to him after he dropped it so I brought it in here." She took the wallet from me, somberly. *"Muchas gracias, Señorita,"* she told me. "I will give it to Señor Rodriguez when he returns." She seemed truly impressed by my act of selflessness. I smiled modestly at her as I turned away to study the brass placard on the wall by the door.

It listed the names of all of the lawyers associated with the firm and I scanned it for one name in particular but there was no Rodriguez listed there, so apparently his connection with the *Señores* Sanchez was not that of an associate.

"Adios." I smiled again at the receptionist as I turned to go and she smiled and waved after me. I hoped that I wasn't leaving her in an awkward spot. Most likely the mystery of the wallet would be dismissed as a mere case of mistaken identity.

CHAPTER FOUR

I sauntered back down Insurgentes for two blocks, feeling well pleased with my efforts, then turned west to get back to the hotel in time to meet up with Father and Rudy. Rudy was in the lobby when I got back but there was no sign of Father.

As though he had read my mind Rudy spoke up from where he was sitting on the sofa, watching the lobby television and munching on some kind of orange crackers from a small plastic bag. "He called to say he's running a little late. Want one?" He held the bag out to me but I shook my head.

"No, thanks." I dropped onto the sofa next to him and we sat together in silence awhile. I observed that he had changed his shoes, shirt, socks and shorts and that his hair had a freshly showered look to it. Squinting thoughtfully at him I also noticed that Rudy had a large square patch of gauze peeping out from the knee of his shorts.

"Sorry about your accident," I remarked and Rudy turned to stare at me in surprise, his face flushing pink.

"Who told you?" He demanded. "Were you watching?" I shook my head.

"No. I noticed you changed your clothes and you're bandaged. To me it looks like you fell off a jet ski or something." Rudy shrugged his shoulders, elaborately casual.

"It was nothing."

"What happened?" I asked, curious.

"Nothing," he repeated, slightly irritated.

"That doesn't look like nothing to me." I pointed at the bandage. Rudy frowned but I persisted. "It almost looks like it might need medical attention, stitches maybe," I remarked, pointedly. It wasn't as though I was exactly *threatening* to tell Father about his accident but Rudy knew what I meant and conceded the point.

"All right. It was an accident. Just a little bump. I sort of hit a wall."

"You hit a wall?" I repeated and he nodded. "Who was she?" I asked.

"Who?" he replied, clearly annoyed with my line of questioning.

"Whoever it was you were watching instead of where you were going," I explained. Rudy seemed to struggle with himself for a moment then he sighed.

"I guess I might have been watching Sandra," he admitted, finally.

"Ahhh, Sandra the Aussie," I repeated.

"And how was your day so far?" Rudy asked me pointedly, changing the subject.

"Well, I was —" I began, intending to tell him of my discovery when Father's voice cut through my words.

"Hey guys!" He strode towards us, silencing my narrative. "Hope you two haven't been waiting long, it took a little longer than I'd expected. You ready to go to Bucerías?" Rudy glanced at me and stood up.

"Sure," he agreed and I stood as well, following as Father led the way briskly to our rental car, a sedan in a rather attractive shade of deep blue. We rolled the windows down to let in a fresh breeze as Father started the engine and pulled onto the road.

The streets in the old part of Puerto Vallarta obviously

dated back to an earlier age and, I must say, the local drivers exhibited a certain flair for navigating them quickly. Father took it more slowly, weaving carefully through assorted traffic and courageous pedestrians crossing the streets.

"So what have the two of you been up to?" Father asked, his eyes meeting mine for a second in the rear view mirror.

"Nothing." Rudy replied just a little too quickly, tugging a little at his shorts to hide the gauze on his knee. He caught my eye and shot me a warning look so I politely refrained from explaining to Father just how Rudy had spent his morning.

"How about you, K.C.?" Father smiled at me, raising an eyebrow. "Did you do anything interesting?" I debated telling him the truth and decided I had nothing to lose.

"You won't believe me," I said, finally.

"How do you know until you tell us?" Father asked, reasonably.

"All right, I'll tell you," I replied slowly. "I found out the name of one of the killers from last night. He was walking down the street so I followed him into an office and got his name from the receptionist." There was silence in the car as Rudy and Father exchanged quick glances. "His name is Rodriguez," I offered loudly, even though nobody had asked me.

"Are you still going on about that whole thing?" Rudy asked with a sigh, not even bothering to turn his head. "You know, you really do have way too much imagination."

"It was not my imagination!" I insisted.

"It was too, Kook Case," he retorted.

"It was real, *Trudy*," I shot back. Rudy hates it when I tease him about his name almost as much as I hate it when he teases me about mine. Father was watching the road and then studied me carefully in the mirror as I slumped back in the seat with a shrug, dismissing the whole thing. "See? I told you you wouldn't believe me."

"It's not that we don't believe you, K.C. honey." Father swerved to avoid a horse-drawn carriage heading for the waterfront. "We believe that *you* believe you saw a murder. But that might not have been what happened. Remember, this is a foreign culture and you have to guard against misinterpreting innocent situations."

"Yeah, right," I muttered. "Misinterpreting." Personally I could hardly see how I would ever be able to misinterpret something like watching someone beat someone else to a pulp then crush his head and drag him out to a car, but I no longer felt like arguing the point. We all lapsed into silence as Father negotiated traffic through the northern part of the city.

The city streets in the newer part of Puerto Vallarta widened gradually. Soon we were part of a long line of cars heading north on Mexico 200. The road from there to Bucerías consisted of an asphalt highway leading to the airport, past the pacific coast campus of the University of Guadalajara to Nuevo Vallarta, and then stretching through kilometer after kilometer of small towns and open fields. The fields seemed surprisingly dry and dusty, until I remembered that the rainy season wouldn't start until June, two months away. The grass looked thirsty in the stiff, hot breeze. We passed a coconut farm, long aisles of palm trees stretching away into the distance, coconuts hanging in great clusters under broad flat leaves.

Father and Rudy were talking in the front seat of the car and I had the back seat all to myself so I stared out the window and thought my own thoughts while looking out at the scenery. I was struck by the pervading coexistence of old and new in Mexico. Rickety wooden outbuildings with thatched palm leaf roofs shared lots with newer concrete and steel structures, making for odd neighbors.

Farther up the road and off to the right I saw a miniature race track where those who were so inclined could rent small race cars and play with one another at being world-famous drivers. The "Mini-Indy 500" turns the boys on, I guess. Two of the cars were speeding around the paved curves as I watched, each trying to out-maneuver the other.

I saw a red and green PeMex gas station on one wall of which someone had painted a bright red heart with the words 'Verónica y Archi' written inside it. (Probably a relic of Jughead's Mexican vacation. Who knew?) About thirty minutes after that Father finally pulled left off the highway into a side street which curved left again and broadened into the central plaza of Bucerías.

Father parked the car along the plaza close to the beach and we all got out, standing on a point which looked out over the waterfront. The ocean stretched before miles of white beach as far as I could see, endless green crystal waves melting on hot sand. A serious wind was blowing off the water, making the palm trees dance and whirl. Fortunately for me my hat was jammed firmly on my head or I would have lost it in the breeze.

"The property in question is down this way," Father told us, having consulted a map provided to him by his client. We took a short flight of stairs to get down to the beach and walked along the beachfront, across sand dunes to get to the acreage marked by a small red square on Father's map. Again I was amazed by the contrasts in Mexico.

A veritable mansion stood before us on our left, with tall white marble pillars supporting a pale gold stucco house two stories tall. It was topped by a white tiled roof and the entire first floor seemed to consist of huge picture windows overlooking the bay. The boundaries of the yard were clearly indicated by a waist-high stone fence topped by sharp barbed wire which stretched along the property line.

On the lot directly adjacent to the mansion stood an ancient, crumbling concrete edifice of what might at one time have been a warehouse. Made of large grey bricks, it was slowly succumbing to the wind and the sun. Huge chunks of daylight showed through where pieces of it had tumbled down to lie in disarray on the ground, overgrown by weeds.

"This is it," Father said, looking it all over with a professional's forgiving eye. "It's perfect, see?" He waved at the land behind the structure. "The property extends fully back along this dry river bed to the road. It has direct access from the highway."

Rudy and I followed in the direction of his wave, studying the tangled jumble of underbrush and crumbling brick which comprised the property line along the river. It didn't exactly look perfect to me, but then I knew that Father was seeing it in terms of what it would become rather than what it already was.

A shadow briefly blocked the sunlight over my head and I looked up in time to see a pelican swoop by. I watched as it hovered effortlessly over the ocean about two hundred yards out from shore then dove straight down to embed itself head and shoulders in the waves. When it popped back up it gulped conspicuously, swallowing the fish it had caught and floated there quietly for a moment before taking to the air again.

"I'd like to take a few pictures, if you two don't mind?" Father was adjusting his camera as he spoke and Rudy and I glanced at each other, rolling our eyes. Father has been known to spend hours when he asks for a few "minutes" to take pictures.

"I think I'll take a walk on the beach," I told Father and Rudy nodded.

"Me too. Want some company, K.C.?" I nodded at him and we left Father there, absorbed in his work. Somewhere nearby a rooster crowed, its song (if you could call it that) seemingly at odds with the hour of the day.

Rudy and I strolled along the white sand beach which sloped gently up from the sea. Every fifty feet or so long, wide piles of rocks stretched along the sand up from the water, where the waves had deposited them like so much luggage from the ocean's restless travels.

I listened to the hissing, sucking gurgle of the water as it pulled away from the rocks, gathering itself for another onslaught on the beach and amused myself by picking up a few of the fist-sized chunks of abalone shell which lay in profusion at my feet. According to the guidebook I'd consulted earlier, the shells were free for the taking so I selected several prime samples and stuffed them into my pocket for future reference.

Rudy was about a hundred yards ahead of me on the beach by then. Having no interest whatsoever in shells, he was heading for a small cluster of thatched grass *palapas* which lined the beach near a group of larger restaurants, where some tourist types were sunbathing.

"Hola, Señorita." I heard a voice behind me and turned to find myself face to face with a girl my own age. She was smiling as she crooked a small tray of hand-carved rock and jade figurines under her arm.

"Hola." I smiled back, watching as she studied me the way I'd studied her. She was about my height with warm brown skin, long glossy dark hair and a friendly smile. She was wearing red shorts and a white sleeveless blouse tucked haphazardly into the waistband of her shorts. On her feet were braided leather sandals like my own, only hers were white in color instead of brown.

"I have carvings, if you like." She proffered the tray

and I was pleased to see among a jumble of carved parrots, dolphins and fish, a set of seven unicorns. The unicorns seemed to be made of some kind of quartz and were graduated in size, from quite tiny to three inches tall.

"These are beautiful," I told her sincerely. "How much? *¿Cuantos pesos?*" She gave me a considering look and flashed a grin at me.

"Good price, fifty pesos," she told me and I nodded.

"*Seguro.* Deal." She put the tray on the sand and began to wrap each unicorn carefully in newspaper for me, spending time on each one so they wouldn't get chipped.

I happened to glance down at the sand behind her and my eye was caught by what looked like a porcupine balloon lying there. I mean, upon closer inspection I could see that it was a dead fish but it was puffed out and covered all over by deadly looking spines which extended about an inch from its body.

"What the heck is that thing?" I exclaimed, pointing at it and the girl paused in her wrapping to turn and look over her shoulder at it.

"Um, it is *pescado*. Fish." She spoke with a shrug and a smile, and I grinned back at her.

"I knew that, but what *kind* of fish is it?" I asked. She searched for the right word and puffed out her cheeks at me.

"Puffer fish." She looked so funny that I giggled. Chuckling, she went back to the task of wrapping the unicorns carefully in newspaper.

"Your English is very good," I told her. She shrugged.

"I sell the carvings to pay for my English lessons." She indicated the contents of her tray with pride and I nodded.

"These really are cool, thanks." She smiled again and, as if on impulse, held out her hand.

"I am Gabriela Velazquez." I shook it warmly and replied,

"And I'm Konstantina Cassandra Flanagan, but my friends call me K.C." We smiled at each other and I experienced one of those moments when you meet a stranger you feel you've known forever.

Gabriela began wrapping the last of the unicorns in a sheet of newspaper and I was opening my mouth to ask her where she lived when suddenly she froze, staring down at the newspaper in her hand as her face went pale beneath her tan.

"Are you O.K.?" I asked, concerned by the sudden stillness which had come over her. She was reading something on the page before her and, bending over to read it myself, I was shocked to see a head and shoulders photograph of the same man I'd seen murdered the night before.

CHAPTER FIVE

The picture had obviously been taken while he was alive and before he had been beaten to the bloody mess I'd last seen. He faced the camera with a shy smile, it looked as though the photo itself might have come from an identification card on file somewhere.

"That's the man I saw last night! Is this today's paper?" I peeked over Gabriela's shoulder to see that it was indeed the morning paper as she continued to read in silence. Her eyes widened and she mumbled in Spanish, with obvious disbelief, "*¿Juan Perez? ¡No es Juan Perez, es Señor David Flores Casteñada!*" She got to her feet, the tray of carvings forgotten as she stared at the photograph.

"You know that guy?" I asked, and something of my intensity got through to her then for she lowered the paper to look at me. "Who is Juan Perez?" I asked, wishing that my Spanish were better. She shook her head and pointed at the picture, replying,

"Juan Perez is, um...John Doe."

"John who?"

Gabriela shook her head, impatient with the process of finding words. Gesturing at the picture she said,

"*Es Señor David Flores Casteñada.*"

"Then who is Juan Perez?" I asked in bewilderment. We gazed at each other in mutual consternation and I sat down abruptly in the sand, narrowly missing the unfortunate puffer fish. Gabriela followed suit and finished reading the article in silence. I left her alone until she folded the paper neatly and tucked it into her tray, apparently gathering herself to leave.

"Wait a minute," I told her. *"Un momentito por favor."* She looked at me somewhat impatiently, clearly wanting to be on her way but I held up a hand. "Please, *por favor.* I saw that man killed last night," I told her, speaking slowly and clearly. *"¿Comprendes? Asasinato.* Two men killed him," I told her, hoping I'd gotten the words right. A frown creased Gabriela's brow and she murmured,

"¿Asasinato?"

I nodded in response.

"Yeah, murdered." I pointed at the photo then picked up a rock from the shoreline and lifted it over my head, bringing it down on a nearby coconut shell left behind by the waves. The shell cracked and splintered in a gruesome display more effective than any words could have been and Gabriela's eyes narrowed.

"You saw this *hombre* murdered? *Es la verdad?*" she asked me, and I nodded again.

"Yes, it's the truth," I assured her grimly.

"No lo creo, I don't believe it." She shook her head slowly, staring at me, *"Una alucinación."*

"I wasn't hallucinating! I saw it happen! Two men killed him," I insisted in the face of her disbelief. She studied me for a moment, then broke into a flood of Spanish so rapid and complex that I couldn't follow her at all. I shook my head.

"No entiendo," I said eventually, when she was finally winding down, and she sighed. Speaking slowly, she held the newspaper out to me and said,

"This paper say he die in a boating, um...*un accidente.*"

"A boating accident?" I shook my head firmly. "Not

even close." I reached for the rock again to demonstrate exactly how I'd seen Señor Casteñada murdered but she quickly held up a hand to forestall my macabre mime show. We sat there in silence for a little while and then she asked,

"¿Por que? Why do they kill him?" I shook my head and spread my hands in the universal gesture of puzzlement.

"I don't know. I just know I saw two men beat him up and take him to a hotel room where they bashed his head." Gabriela nodded.

"¿Dos hombres?" She held up two fingers and I nodded.

"Yeah, there were two of them. Who was Señor Casteñada?" I asked and Gabriela replied,

"He is a fisherman."

"Was a fisherman," I corrected absently. I couldn't see Rudy anywhere nearby and suddenly the beach seemed very deserted. I waved at the road leading down the river gully where I knew Father was taking his pictures. I wanted him to see the newspaper article for himself.

"¿Vamos, amiga?" I suggested and Gabriela nodded at me, apparently comfortable with the notion of accompanying me that far and we followed the river bed back toward where I thought Father would be. I heaved a huge sigh of relief when I saw him standing by the road, deeply engaged in conversation with a middle aged man wearing white pants and jacket.

"¡Padre!" Gabriela exclaimed just as I yelped,

"Father!"

We stopped to look at each other in mutual surprise while our respective fathers gave us smiles from where they stood.

"Hey K.C., how was the beach? Find any good shells?" my Father called, his relaxed stance and open demeanor about as different from my own mood as possible. "Where's Rudy?"

he asked me, his smile fading into a frown. "I thought you two were going to stick together." I shook my head.

"He's up the beach near that restaurant," I pointed. "He, uh, found something he liked." The last time I'd seen him Rudy had been talking to a girl with long, black hair selling cold drinks under a thatched *palapa*.

"Look, Father, I have to talk to you about something," I began urgently, meaning to tell him about how I'd discovered the identity of the man I'd seen killed but I was interrupted as Father introduced me to Gabriela's father.

"K.C., this is Señor Augustín Velazquez." I bit back my flood of words and shook the man's hand. He was of medium height, had thick curly hair and warm eyes and I could see where Gabriela had gotten her friendly smile.

"I am pleased to meet you," he smiled at me, "and this is my daughter, Gabriela." He continued. "Gabriela, *Señor* James Flanagan. Rudy strolled up to join us at that point, wearing a brand new pair of hot pink heart-shaped sunglasses and a broad smile, so we introduced him to the Velazquez'. There were more handshakes all around while Gabriela and I looked at each other slightly impatiently.

After this third and final round of introductions Gabriela handed her father the newspaper containing the article we had stumbled across. He stared down at it, all traces of good humor vanishing from his face as he perused the contents.

"Is something wrong?" Father asked, his gaze sharpening at this transition. Señor Velazquez showed him the page and remarked,

"A good friend of mine has had the boating accident." His English was very nearly perfect.

"That's the same man I saw killed last night!" I spoke up insistently. "That's what I wanted to tell you. Look there, see? Do you recognize him? You saw his face too, remember,

Rudy?" I grabbed the paper and gave it an emphatic shake right under Rudy's nose until he frowned at me and pulled away.

"I saw a hat on the head of a drunk guy who was being carried to the car by his friends," Rudy replied, tersely. "Quit kidding around, K.C."

"I'm not kidding! You have to believe me, that's the same guy I saw killed last night." Father and Señor Velazquez were watching me with genuine alarm and Father interjected, "I suggest that we discuss this over dinner."

"But…" I began and he forestalled my protests with a raised hand.

"I don't mean to ignore your concerns, K.C. but I think we'll be more comfortable discussing it in the shade, over food. The last thing we need is a case of heat stroke and I don't know about you but I'm hungry," he added and I could hardly argue with his logic.

"You will come to my restaurant." Señor Velazquez grinned and clapped Father on the back. "We have very good food. It is right there, at the end of the street." Señor Velazquez pointed toward a building of white clapboard topped by a red tiled roof and Father accepted immediately. The two of them headed off down the narrow cobbled street toward the restaurant. Gabriela and I shrugged at each other then followed. Out of the corner of my eye, I was displeased to notice Rudy checking Gabriela out. Hormones rule the world, I guess.

The restaurant was built right out over the beach below and strands of seashells shimmered like curtains in its airy windows. We were hosted by a veritable crowd of waiters who rushed to seat us at a table on the elongated terrace where the waves seemed to break directly below us.

Despite my preoccupation with recent developments I wasn't so distracted that I couldn't enjoy my meal of savory scallops in a light butter and garlic sauce. I even had several slices of a flat pan bread piled high with creamy guacamole before anyone mentioned the murder again.

"Now, K.C." Father pushed back his plate and steepled his fingers, "I think we need to talk about this."

"You're telling me," I sighed.

"You've made some pretty serious allegations today and before we discuss the matter any further I want you to be sure that you mean what you tell me, all right?" Father's gaze was detached, and I could see he was functioning in a semi-professional capacity.

"I saw the man in the picture get murdered by two men in a hotel room across the street last night. They carried him out to their car and drove him away, remember? I know it looked like he'd been drinking, at least to the hotel guard who checked, but I saw them bash him in the head," I told him.

"Are you sure you recognize him as the man in this photograph?" Father asked me. Señor Velazquez leaned forward as I nodded.

"As positive as I can be." Once again, I related the sequence of events which led me to believe I had witnessed a murder and when I had finished everyone at the table wore grim faces. "And the name of one of the guys who killed him is Rodriguez." I stopped there. Gabriela gasped and repeated.

"¿Señor Rodriguez?"

"¿Señor Angel Rodriguez?" Her father spoke at the same time, fixing me with a penetrating stare.

"I don't know what his first name is, I only know his last name," I told him.

"And how would you know that?" He wanted to know. I took a deep breath and explained,

"Because I followed him this morning. He went into a law firm and after he left I asked the receptionist for his name.

Do you know him? Rodriguez, I mean?" It was my turn to be puzzled as Gabriela and Señor Velazquez exchanged glances. A look both thoughtful and worried crossed Señor Velazquez' face and he told us,

"There is a Señor Rodriguez who lives here in Bucerías," Velazquez said slowly. "He works for Señor Ravalos' Construction and Shipping Company. He is a very powerful man in Bucerías."

"It might not be the same man," Father pointed out reasonably. "There are many people with the name Rodriguez in this part of the world."

"That is true." Señor Velazquez nodded thoughtfully, seeming to reconsider his earlier conclusion. "I will go to the police about this first thing tomorrow morning," he promised us. "I will tell them who Casteñada is and that there was a witness to his murder." He turned to me, a shadow of doubt crossing his face. "You would be willing to tell the police about what you saw? I glanced briefly at Father then nodded.

"I sure would," I informed him.

There was a thoughtful silence at our table for a moment then Father launched into the standard lecture on travel safety, outlining what I already knew. Don't follow sinister strangers, stay on well-lighted public streets, etc. I listened in resigned silence until Father concluded his lecture with a speech about how Rudy and I should try to stick together more, (at which point Rudy and I exchanged dark looks) and about how we were to try and stay out of trouble.

I would have argued that I was not the one getting into trouble, that it wasn't *my* fault if someone just happened to kill someone else while I watched, but it didn't seem prudent so I kept silent, nodding in all the right places.

After that, the conversation shifted to less sinister topics as Father and Señor Velazquez led the conversation back to business and for the next half hour they discussed the beneficial effect that development would have on Bucerías.

From what Señor Velazquez told us, the development planned by Father's company was being hailed by the local people as a good thing because an additional hotel would consequently mean a new market for the fresh fish caught by local fishermen.

Father mentioned the competing offer on the property very delicately, asking only if Señor Velazquez knew of anyone in town who may have had other plans for the property.

"There has been no one else interested in this property, only your company." Señor Velazquez replied thoughtfully, rubbing his chin. "It has been deserted for many years, ever since a fire destroyed the building there."

Father nodded. "But you've heard no talk about anyone buying it?" Señor Velazquez shook his head.

"Not a word."

"I see." Father changed the subject as we finished the rest of our meals. "Rudy, I was hoping that you and K.C. would do me a favor tomorrow afternoon and go see a tourist spot south of town called Chico's Paradise. My client might be thinking of doing something similar with the property here and I was supposed to research it but I won't have time. I'll be attending meetings instead." Gabriela's face brightened somewhat as she repeated,

"Chico's Paradise? I heard it is very nice." Father and Señor Velazquez exchanged quick glances and I suggested, "Why don't you come with us tomorrow morning? We could all go together if you like."

"Good idea."

"*Es muy bien.*" Gabriela and I shared a smile, enjoying a brief respite from the grim mood which had enveloped us all.

The sun was sinking low on the water by the time we pushed back our plates. Señor Velazquez had ordered everything on the menu for us and I had tried everything so I felt as though I could barely move.

"Feel like dancing?" Gabriela teased me as a group of musicians began to set up their instruments on a small stage at the end of the terrace.

"I sure do," Rudy interrupted, grinning mischievously at Gabriela and she blushed.

"Don't let him start on you, Gabriela," I warned her, "he's the biggest flirt in the world."

"I am not," Rudy protested indignantly. "I just like getting to know people. Dance?" He invited her again and she shyly accepted, before I could point out that Rudy inevitably got to know only young, pretty girls, and lots of them. I watched in some amusement from our table as the two of them tried to find dance steps which matched the music, a difficult task as the music seemed to be an interesting hybrid of polka and traditional Mexican folk music.

What followed then was nothing less than a fiesta. The musicians played enthusiastically and the restaurant's patrons came to our table to greet Señor Velazquez and to meet his guests. Father and the company he represented were acclaimed by all. There were smiles all around, lots of beer and even more laughter as a small crowd of people gathered in the restaurant to celebrate the end of another day.

I strolled past a group of dancers, into the restaurant proper and up a flight of polished wooden stairs to the upper balcony, partly to look at the view but mostly to escape the dancing. The soft murmur of a woman's voice drifted to me as I leaned over the railing and I became still, listening as a familiar name caught my attention.

"Casteñada was... (here a wave broke on the beach

54

with a booming roar, drowning out the next few words.)...I'm afraid. Promise me you will say nothing...*¿por favor*? You must promise!" There was a long pause after the woman finished speaking then a man's voice drifted to my ears,

"Shhh, say no more. We will talk of it another time." Their voices faded away as the two of them rejoined the party and I slipped away from the railing, taking the stairs two at time on my way back down to the main floor.

I had hoped to catch a glimpse of them and maybe ask the woman what she had meant when she'd cautioned her apparent lover to say nothing but I was out of luck, there was no sign of the two I'd heard talking. They had long since mingled with the crowd and there was no way I could tell them from the rest of the people there. Soberly I crossed the room to rejoin the others.

"I think we'd better head home." Father glanced at his watch in surprise. "It was good to meet all of you. We'll take good care of Gabriela tomorrow, I promise." Father shook hands with Señor Velazquez and he, in turn, assured us that he had every confidence in us. Then Rudy, Father and I headed back to where we had parked the rental car.

"Gabriela seems like a nice girl," Rudy commented and I shook my head resignedly at him in the darkness. All girls seem nice to Rudy and apparently Gabriela was no exception. "And her father is nice too," he added, as an afterthought.

"That he is." Father seemed pleasantly surprised to have made such good friends without expecting to. "It will be a pleasure working with him in the future. I'll have to see if he'd consider some kind of partnership with the hotel when we build it." Father frowned a little at the road before him and added, "That is, if we build it." I knew he was remembering the problem of the competing offer on the property.

We made the rest of the journey home in silence and Father parked the car in a space conveniently open directly in front of the hotel. I was stepping out of the car and straightening up when the headlights of another parked car suddenly sprang to life directly across from me and its engine roared. It was facing the wrong way down the street and heading right toward me.

"K.C.!" Rudy shouted, "Look out!" I stared at the oncoming headlights for a fraction of a second then dove back inside the rental car, sliding across the seat just in time to avoid the oncoming vehicle which swept by so closely that its mirror slammed the door shut behind me, leaving a long scratch in the side of our car.

"K.C., are you all right?" Father and Rudy crossed the courtyard to my side in an instant, wrenching the car door open.

"I'm fine," I lied shakily, swallowing hard as I climbed out. I glanced cautiously around in case the driver of the car changed his mind and came back to have another go at me. That had been too close for comfort.

"That crazy fool!" Rudy muttered, helping me out of the car with a gentleness and concern he doesn't usually show me. "Probably drunk off his..." he caught Father's eye and left the sentence unfinished.

"Did you get a look at the license plate number?" I asked them both and they shook their heads regretfully.

"No, sorry, it was going too fast," Father told me.

"Way too fast," Rudy muttered wrathfully. I tried to think of something to say which would alleviate both their concern and my own but couldn't. I had nearly met with an untimely demise at the hands of what was probably a drunk driver and the experience had left me thoroughly shaken.

We went inside the hotel somberly, heading for the

sanctuary of our rooms at the top of the stairs. I don't want to make it seem like I'm a coward or anything but I must admit that even when I reached my room my heart was still pounding in my chest like I'd run some kind of marathon. Father paused at my door and studied me with deep concern.

"Are you sure you're all right?" he asked me, for the third time and for the third time I nodded back at him.

"I'm fine," I told him again.

"Well, all right," he seemed reluctant to let me out of his sight, "but remember if you need anything Rudy and I are right next door." We parted company and I locked the door behind me, bolting it shut and hooking the chain too, just to be safe.

The doors to the balcony from my room were closed, just the way I'd left them earlier in the day, with sliding metal bars across them which locked them like big bolts. I checked them to be sure that they were still securely shut then drew the curtains fully closed across the windows before I cautiously turned on the lights.

I sat down to take inventory of my situation. The more I thought about it the more I began to wonder if what had almost happened to me had really been an accident. It began to seem like more than mere coincidence that one night I'd seen a man murdered and the next I was almost turned into a statistic on hit-and-run deaths.

Luckily I have good reflexes and had been able to avoid the collision, but maybe next time I wouldn't be so fortunate. Right about then it occurred to me that perhaps staying at the Hotel Fontana Del Mar was a little too risky for my health and I headed for the door, intending to ask Father to get us out of there on the double.

I realized in time to stop myself that if in fact Rodriguez had it in for me, he would likely be far more familiar with

Puerto Vallarta than we were and would easily be able to follow three strangers in town, no matter where we went. Moving out of the hotel would do no good whatsoever.

The phrase 'you can run but you can't hide' popped into my mind and I could only hope that my suspicions about the near-miss accident were way off base, because I was starting to feel like I would never get a chance to have the normal vacation I'd fantasized about, swimming in the surf and falling asleep in the sun.

I got into bed in the darkness, making sure that my travel flashlight was on the stand beside my bed. Then, despite my certainty that I wouldn't sleep a wink, I closed my eyes and slept without waking until dawn.

CHAPTER SIX

The next day dawned bright and beautiful of course, but not even blue skies blazing overhead eased my worries from the night before. I showered and dressed then opened the balcony door cautiously to the sound of Rudy's solid tenor bellowing out a funky rendition of Blue Suede Shoes. This is Rudy's standard morning shower song and although I doubt that Elvis Presley himself would have recognized Rudy's version, it is effective in its own way. Father strolled out onto the balcony and seeing me standing there, smiled.

"Good morning," he greeted me. "How are you?"

I smiled and replied, "Fine," just as Rudy bellowed out the last verse and joined us on the balcony. Clad in a white cotton robe, he was vigorously rubbing his head dry with a towel.

"Evening, folks." He assumed a hokey American accent which twanged from his nose like a badly tuned guitar. "And how are y'all tonight? I wanna thank y'all for coming out to see me." Rudy seized a corner of the towel and spoke into it like a microphone; he can be pretty silly sometimes. Abruptly he dropped his clownish pose and studied me.

"You O.K., sis?" he asked me with genuine brotherly concern. "After last night and all?" I nodded and shrugged simultaneously, really touched by his sincere interest in my well-being.

"Yeah, I'm fine, Rudy."

"Good." He then reverted to his usual obnoxious self, snapping his damp towel at my leg.

Once Rudy had finished getting dressed we three strolled east along Badillo street to a pancake house, having decided to go for a more North American spin on things as far as breakfast was concerned. The coffee there smelled excellent and I even ordered a cup of the stuff myself, even though I don't usually drink it since it makes me sort of hyper. In any case I figured I was on edge enough anyway that drinking some wouldn't actually make all that much difference.

For despite my assurances to Rudy and my Father, I was beginning to feel plenty nervous about the things that had been happening lately and about how they boded ill for the future. I mean from all signs matters were probably going to get worse before they got better. I poured fresh cream into my coffee and sipped it thoughtfully, sitting with my back to the wall as I watched the sidewalk in front of the pancake house.

"Hey look, K.C." Rudy had been perusing the English version of the Puerto Vallarta Daily newspaper and now he pointed to an article he had been reading. "It's about Casteñada." I nearly dropped my coffee in my haste to take the newspaper from him and Father slid his chair around the table so that we could read the paper together.

There was another photo of Señor Casteñada smiling at us from the page, the same one which had been used in the paper the day before, accompanied by a short article about his death. One sentence in particular grabbed my attention:

"...the death of local fisherman, David Flores Casteñada, is being investigated for signs of foul play. Police are asking anyone with information to step forward." I skimmed the article rapidly.

There was more along the same lines, about how Casteñada had been found floating facedown in the water of the bay the previous day, about how his death, first presumed to be an accident was now considered suspicious enough to warrant an investigation by the police and more about his life and his surviving family.

"It does look like there might be more to Casteñada's death than a mere boating accident," Father conceded gravely as we handed the paper back to Rudy. "But that doesn't necessarily mean that there isn't another explanation for what you saw, K.C. Still, I think we should go to the police," he added and I nodded my agreement.

"When?" I asked and he steepled his fingers over his cup of coffee.

"We'll go together, this afternoon." I felt immensely relieved that I would finally be able to drop the responsibility for the investigation of Casteñada's murder into the capable hands of the local police.

"Are we ready to go?" Father paid the bill when it came, then turned to me with a serious expression on his face while we waited for the waiter to make change from the bill Father had given him. "K.C. I want you to promise me that you'll be very careful from here on in, all right?" I nodded back slowly as he went on, "That means don't go following sinister strangers, in fact don't go anywhere at all without telling me or Rudy exactly where you'll be, promise?" I nodded again, more reluctantly.

Don't get me wrong, I was well aware of the need for caution, but it didn't seem fair to me that just because there were a couple of nasty dudes in town *I* should be the one to suffer a loss of personal freedom. I could tell that Father was waiting for my reply so I said grudgingly,

"All right, I promise."

"And you, Rudy, promise me that you'll stay close to K.C., keep an eye on her." There was no arguing with Father's tone and Rudy nodded, eyeing me askance.

"I promise." He agreed and I knew he would give me a hard time about the situation later. I didn't have long to wait.

"*Now* look what you've done," Rudy muttered as we walked back to the hotel.

"Me?" I turned an outraged look on him, whispering. "None of this is *my* fault. All I was doing was minding my own business when…"

"Yeah, right," he snorted. "You, minding your own business? It'll never happen." He was being so completely unfair that I was tempted to kick him in the shins but I have long since outgrown such childish displays of temper and so I contented myself with sticking my tongue out at him.

"There's no reason why you two can't still have fun." Father smiled over his shoulder at us, utterly unaware of this exchange. "You guys always get along so well together, it should be easy for you to find things you both want to do."

"Oh yeah, like flirting with everything that's female and breathing," I remarked sarcastically, "that's just *tons* of fun."

"Beats the heck out of following creepy strangers," Rudy observed, "but we won't be doing any more of that now will we, Kook Case?" By this time we had reached the hotel and I spotted Gabriela waiting for us in the lobby so I simply ignored his attempt to insult me.

"*Buenos dias.*" Gabriela smiled at us as we joined her.

"*Buenos dias.*" Rudy shouldered me aside to greet her first with a big, welcoming smile. Taking her hand, he bowed low over it theatrically, looking a lot like an actor from a B-grade movie. "You look very beautiful," he murmured, his eyes intent on her face.

"Hi there, Gabriela," I put in, "you'll have to excuse Rudy for grabbing at you like that, he's coming down with a tropical fever of some sort. It's making him a little dizzy."

"Fever?" Gabriela pulled her hand away, trying to seem like she wasn't in any hurry to do so. "What kind of fever?" Rudy scowled at me as I continued blithely,

"It's nothing serious, it just affects his ability to reason. You'll hardly notice any difference in him."

"Oh?" Gabriela looked from one to the other of us, a small smile hovering on her lips. "You are having the joke at me, I think."

"Don't mind K.C., she's always imagining things," Rudy remarked pointedly, "seeing things, too." We smiled dangerously at each other and Gabriela laughed out loud at us.

"You are just like my little sister and brother. Always teasing each another." Father nodded at her remark.

"That about sums it up, all right. These two are always kidding around." He glanced at his watch, a small frown replacing his smile. "Well, I have to be going now. Remember what I told you, stay together and be sure you let each other know where you'll be if one of you goes somewhere." Thus cautioning us against the evils of the world, Father left us to our own devices.

"Next stop, Chico's Paradise," Rudy informed Gabriela and me with a grin. We had caught the public bus at the corner of Badillo and Insurgentes. We'd taken the one going to Mismaloya since a quick consultation of the map had told us that for two and a half pesos it would drop us off nearest the road leading to Chico's Paradise.

It had been easy to figure out exactly which of the many buses we wanted because they all had their destinations painted in white letters across the upper parts of their windshields. The bus was fairly crowded, even though it was only 9:30 in the morning. To me it looked as though many of our fellow passengers were on their way to work.

We traveled south out of town along Mexico 200. The winding highway was set into a hillside which slanted sharply up and back from the sea. Whereas our trip to Bucerías the day before had taken us north, across more or less flat plains, we were heading the other way now, through mountainous territory.

The road twisted and turned every hundred yards or so, hugging the side of the mountains like a lover's arm, and on one side of us there was a rocky hillside to which straggly-looking trees were clinging painfully. On the other side was a steep drop to the far-reaching blue waters of the *Bahía de Banderas* below.

I stared fascinated out over the water of the bay, glancing behind us every so often to see if we had been followed. I tried not to be obvious about my observation of the road behind us but I must have looked like a jack-in-the-box, swiveling around in my seat every two minutes to study the road while Rudy flirted outrageously with Gabriela.

"That's a really pretty necklace you're wearing," he told her, twisting all the way around in the seat in front of us to favor her with his patented charm. Gabriela smiled at him shyly.

"My mother made it," she told him and he admired the beadwork, commenting astutely on the craftsmanship. I eyed the two of them askance. I have seen Rudy in action before. When he flirts he takes himself quite seriously and I had a sudden vision of him whisking Gabriela away just when I wanted to talk to her alone.

I was dying to ask her more about Señor Rodriguez but I didn't want to do so while Rudy was around since he'd only make fun of me and discourage Gabriela from telling me what she knew. My only hope was to separate the two of them long enough to get her alone but Rudy was making it plain he intended to stick to Gabriela like a stamp to an envelope. I cleared my throat loudly.

"So, how is Sandra these days?" I asked Rudy loudly and he glared at me as I reminded him, "You remember her, don't you? That gorgeous blond girl you met on the beach the other day?" Rudy flushed a little and shrugged off my remark.

"Oh, her. I'm surprised you remember her name, I hardly even spoke with her. What was her name? Samantha?" He smiled beguilingly at Gabriela and changed the subject adroitly. "Gabriela. Your name is nice. Does it mean anything?"

"I was named for my mother." She nodded.

"Hmmm, that's right," I said thoughtfully. "You haven't dated anyone named Gabriela yet, have you Rudy?" He gave me a chilling stare as I went on, counting on the fingers of both hands. "Let's see, there was Betty, Angela, Rikki, Genevieve, Penny, Harriet, Joan and Stephanie." Gabriela's brows arched in delicate surprise and her dimples began to show as I finished. "Did I miss any of your girlfriends from last winter semester, Rudy?"

He gazed at me with a dark promise in his eyes and there was what you might call tension in the air. After that, Gabriela looked out the window and Rudy faced forward, making no further attempt to flirt with her for the duration of the trip.

I kept glancing behind us, just in case anyone was following, but I didn't see any suspicious looking cars from the rear window of the bus and after a while I began to relax. The near accident of the night before had probably been just that — an accident. At least, that was what I wanted to believe and in the clear light of day it began to seem more probable.

We passed quite a few luxury hotels along the way to our destination and I noticed a lot of condominiums and townhouses built into the hillside. I began to understand where all the people on the bus with us were employed, since they disembarked in small groups each time it stopped near such an establishment.

As Father had instructed him to, Rudy took pictures and jotted observations in his notebook to record the various types of property development efforts in the area. Gabriela studied his face surreptitiously while he was thus occupied and I saw her smile a little when he brushed his thick curly chestnut hair back from his eyes. I sighed resignedly. A lot of girls get that way around Rudy.

We crossed several bridges spanning mountain streams which ran down from the hills to the ocean below. Road signs advertising beaches below caught my eye and I suggested that we stop on the way back to investigate the ruins of the movie set for the film *Night of the Iguana* at Mismaloya beach. Rudy unbent sufficiently towards me to admit that it seemed like a good plan.

We got off the bus in front of the Mismaloya Hotel and caught a cab to take us the last part of the way to Chico's Paradise. As we were traveling around a narrow turn in the road the taxi driver hit the brakes quite suddenly halfway down a steep hill and pointed at something in the road with a gap-toothed grin.

"Es un iguana." He pointed and we saw a big, fat, gray, two foot long lizard in the middle of the road. It stared blandly at us for a moment then moved languidly across the road into the underbrush there and disappeared from sight. The driver shook his head and accelerated, taking us the last half mile to Chico's Paradise.

Chico's was a delightful river area where tourists swam in deep pools of water carved into giant boulders by millenia of gentle river rapids. I was enchanted by the crystal green clarity of the water and when Rudy and Gabriela decided that a swim sounded good I didn't argue but gladly joined them.

We splashed each other and swam in the pools of cool water under the hot sun, and I must say it was the perfect blend of activity and relaxation that I hadn't known I'd needed. We ended up tired and happy, sprawled across the tops of sun-warmed boulders by the water's edge, watching the local kids diving for coins the tourists were throwing into the water from the restaurant railing high above us. "Meester, meester, 'trow money, hey, hey, 'trow money!" I began to think that it might be possible for me to have a normal, fun vacation after all.

"How about some lunch?" Rudy suggested not long after his stomach had growled audibly. Gabriela rolled over on her side, and we all studied our options. We agreed unanimously on the large restaurant from where coins were still raining down, the one built directly over the water in a series of steps conforming to the natural structure of the rocks.

We crossed a narrow rock footbridge, scrambled over two boulders and found ourselves at the foot of a broad stone staircase leading high up into the shade provided by the immense thatched roof of the restaurant. A waiter seated us on the main floor and I spotted a large blue-green macaw perched on the wooden hand rail next to a deserted table.

"*Los caballeros.*" Gabriela grinned as two more macaws strolled along the railing toward the table, shoving the first bird aside amiably as they took its spot on the perch and stretched out their iridescent wings for our admiration.

I watched in amusement as one of the macaws sidled closer to an older, toad-like man with a nasty face who was sipping a beer and talking to a very deferential waiter. The bird then hopped over the man and landed on the back of an empty chair at the table. Leaning over with practiced efficiency, it snatched a piece of tortilla from a side dish and flew to the rafters overhead with a great squawk. The triumphant bird proceeded to drop little bits of tortilla onto the enraged toad-man below until more waiters hurried over to shoo it away, and apologize effusively to the red-faced, and evidently very important customer. It was quite a scene.

The food arrived and was delicious. I sampled tacos, quesadillas, and chimichangas in fresh *salsa* while Rudy had beef burritos. Gabriela opted for the fish filet and nobody said much of anything to anyone for quite some time as we did justice to our meals.

"You swim very well, Gabriela," Rudy complimented her over his fruit salad.

"I live by the ocean," she replied simply. "Where do you come from?"

"Montreal, Canada." Rudy informed her.

"Mon-tray-al. ¡Caramba!" Gabriela was impressed. "French." She grinned impishly at him. "Your *inglés* is very good. Do you speak any other languages?" Rudy smiled back modestly.

"Besides Spanish and French, I speak some German, a little Gaelic, and now I'm studying Russian in school. I am the master of many tongues," he told her, assuming an attitude of world-weary savoir-faire.

"Yeah, and most of them aren't even his," I said with a straight face, making a joke that only Rudy understood. "He gets a lot of practice, believe me."

"Shut up, K.C." Rudy glowered at me as Gabriela watched us indulgently, amused by our antics even if she didn't understand all of our words.

"Do you travel a lot?" She asked us both and Rudy answered, "Oh my, yes. We've been all over the world. I've always found travel so broadening." He leaned back in his chair, Mr. Sophisticated.

"Yeah, especially the 'broad' part" I said sweetly and turned to include Gabriela in my smile. "Rudy is what you might call 'broad' minded." Rudy shook his head at Gabriela.

"You'll have to forgive K.C., Gabriela," he said impatiently, "she's just an immature child of fourteen." Gabriela's smile faded as she glanced at me. She and I were the exact same age and Rudy recognized his slip immediately. "Not that being young necessarily means being childish," he backpedalled hastily. "Take you, for example, you're very mature for your age." He smiled beguilingly at Gabriela, who she looked at me with amusement.

Suddenly, my eyes were drawn to an arm in a dark shirt, gesticulating wildly in the face of the fat, toad-like man who had now left his table and was disdainfully tossing coins over the railing to the urchins diving into the river pools below. As my jaw dropped, recognizing that the arm belonged to Señor Rodriguez, several things happened all at once.

Rudy and Gabriela noticed my stare and were about to ask me about it when Rodriguez, as if he felt my eyes on him, turned abruptly in our direction and glared. The fat man also looked over to us across the twenty or so tables that separated us, but grabbed Rodriguez by the arm and whispered in his ear, then turned and continued the conversation.

Rodriguez seemed now to ignore us, but it still gave me the chills and with Rudy and Gabriela raising their eyebrows, I quickly got the waiter's attention and left a large bill to pay for our lunch. Waving a hand to indicate that I was not interested in getting the change, I bolted up and charged out of the restaurant, followed by a bewildered Rudy and a totally mystified Gabriela. As we left the restaurant, a taxi was discharging several American tourists and we jumped in and took off as fast as a five hundred-peso note could carry us.

CHAPTER SEVEN

I didn't feel like talking about it to Rudy, so I pre-empted his question with a quick, "Later. Zip it for now," and we directed the driver to let us out about thirty minutes away, in front of the Mismaloya Hotel on the outskirts of Vallarta. A short walk down a cobbled road beside yet another mountain river took us to a wide expanse of white beach dotted with outboard boats for hire.

"Alright! Snorkeling." Rudy observed with deep satisfaction, watching as one such boat left with a cargo of tourists wearing flippers and masks, heading for the rocky islands several hundred yards away. From where we were standing I could see that the waves had carved huge arches under the islands so that it was possible for a boat to pass directly below them. Hence their name, *Los Arcos*.

Out about three hundred yards from the beach there were already several tour boats floating gently on the water while their passengers donned diving gear and dove overboard. I saw a flock of pelicans sitting on the rocks behind them, watching the antics of these humans with what might have been pitying stares.

"Would you like to try it?" Rudy asked Gabriela and she nodded, her face lighting up with a smile. "Good, then let's go," my older brother said. "You want to come too, K.C.?" he added these words as an obvious afterthought and I bit my lip, shaking my head, still trembling from what had happened at the end of lunch at Chico's Paradise.

"Why don't you two go ahead and go snorkeling. I think I'd like to check out the ruins of the movie set right over there on the left." I pointed to the opposite end of the small bay where a long peninsula of rock supported part of the crumbling ruins of the set built for the movie which had made Puerto Vallarta famous.

Gabriela wavered somewhat at my words as though she felt bad about leaving me alone and would accompany me instead, but I could tell that what she really wanted to do was go snorkeling with Rudy and so I insisted that she do so. There seemed little point in trying to force a private talk with her at that moment anyway.

"Try not to get into any trouble while we're gone, K.C." Rudy went into condescending older brother mode. "Remember what Father told us."

"Yeah, and don't *you* get anyone into trouble either," I shot back, right over Gabriela's head.

Rudy and Gabriela joined the next boat load of people heading out to the rocks and I walked slowly south along the beach. A rocky path led up over a gentle hill at the far end of the cove and I followed it down the other side to see the crumbling stone ruins of the set of the movie, *Night of the Iguana*. Weather-beaten and worn, they were mere skeletal reminders of what the set must have looked like.

One or two of the buildings had been adorned by graffiti which had long since faded in the sun, but I was able to make out the words *¡viva la cerveza!* scrawled enthusiastically across one wall. The set looked ancient, which was surprising since it had been built for the movie filmed there by John Huston in the early 1960s, a mere thirty-odd years ago.

I climbed cautiously and quietly into one of the ruined buildings, trying to imagine the American playwright, Tennessee Williams, the director, John Huston, and the movie stars themselves, Richard Burton, Deborah Kerr and Ava Gardner, all hanging out and admiring the view from the very spot where I was standing.

As I had read it, the success of the movie had been a turning point in the history of Puerto Vallarta. Elizabeth Taylor and Richard Burton had fallen in love just before this film, on the set of *Cleopatra,* and gotten married in Montreal (my town!). But they lived together in Puerto Vallarta while Burton shot *Iguana*, and eventually bought the house. Their glamorous movie friends had come by the droves to join the two lovers in their tropical paradise and thus Puerto Vallarta had gotten its reputation for being such a cool city.

Something rattled in the distance and I whirled, reminded of the solitude of the place in one adrenaline-charged moment. I listened intently and for a moment there was nothing, then there was the sound that gravel makes when crunched under someone's shoes. A bird sang in the stillness and I held my breath. Another soft crunch.

I froze and looked around me as the unseen person drew nearer. It might have been my imagination but it seemed to me that whoever he or she was (and in my mind it was more likely to be a he, with a name starting with the letter 'R'), they were taking great pains to be quiet. An ordinary tourist would have come strolling down the road, making a normal racket and maybe even talking or whistling but not this person.

Each footstep I heard was gentle and there were pauses between them, as if the other were stopping to listen for me the way I was for him. I felt the hair lift all along the back of my neck as I realized that I was trapped. I knew of only one way to get back to the relative safety of the beach and other people, but that way was blocked by my pursuer.

I turned this way and that, silently evaluating my

options. Not good. I couldn't go back out of the old building the way I had come in, since I would be immediately visible to whoever was out there. I didn't want to try and hide farther inside the structure itself either. The flooring underfoot seemed unsafe and the whole structure had a rickety look as though it might fall over in a stiff wind. Besides I'll always take my chances on running rather than hiding if I'm forced to choose.

My only chance at escaping detection hinged on being able to leave through the back of the building just as the other person came looking for me at the front. I waited as the footsteps drew nearer, trying to time them as well as I could. A drop of sweat trickled clean down my nose and I didn't even move to brush it away.

As the other person came close enough for me to hear his breathing, I began to take steps toward the open back door of the building, putting my feet down carefully exactly when the other person did and hoping that the noise I made would be covered. As it turned out, I was saved by the cavalry.

"I think the ruins are this way, Charles." A woman's voice drifted over the hill toward me followed by the sound of a man's voice replying,

"Yes Mabel, I'll be right there, dear. I just wanted to have another look at the arches." The man and woman topped the crest of the hill together. Plump and middle-aged, they looked better to me than a life preserver looked to a drowning sailor. I heard a man's voice curse in Spanish behind me and then the sound of someone walking rapidly directly toward where I stood. I had no choice but to make my move.

"Help!" I shouted, sprinting for the back door, and I left the ruined building just as my pursuer entered at the front. I caught a glimpse behind me of the dark, wiry figure I so feared, then I turned to run and heard him curse again as he saw me leave. "Help!" I shouted again as I ran toward my fellow tourists and the man stepped forward, concerned. "What seems to be the trouble, young lady?" he asked me kindly.

"A man is following me, back there." I pointed at the ruins and they followed my direction of my finger. The ruins were quiet behind me. No one had followed my mad flight into the open.

"Where is he, honey?" the woman asked me. "I don't see anyone." She was right, there was no one there. *Nada*. The ruins looked as deserted as ever, only the sound of waves pounding the rocks below broke the stillness.

"Well, he *was* there," I muttered uneasily, keeping an eye on the surrounding bushes while my heart beat like a runaway train. "He couldn't have just vanished into thin air." The man and woman looked at each other then at me, plainly nonplussed.

"I'd be happy to look into it for you, dear." The man grasped his cane firmly and squared his shoulders. "You two ladies just wait right here for me." He was about to set off, bound to investigate the ruins.

"No don't bother, really, it's all right." I shook my head at him, alarmed at the thought of him confronting alone whatever danger might lurk there. The man looked faintly relieved as I added, "I might have been mistaken, I guess."

"Do you want to call someone for help?" His wife offered after a pause for reflection. I shook my head and waved down at the beach below us.

"My brother is over there with my friend, snorkeling. I think I'll just go find him now. Sorry to bother you." I left before they could lecture me about the dangers of heat stroke and its accompanying hallucinations.

I walked quickly back the way I had come, wondering to myself what had just happened. The closer I came to the reassuring string of restaurants along the waterfront and the tourists peacefully nursing their cool drinks, the more I found myself doubting my own interpretation of events.

Was it possible that I was imagining things, the way Rudy had accused me of doing? After all, I'd felt pretty paranoid ever since the night before but I still didn't even know if that whole car thing was a deliberate attack on my life or just a drunk driver.

The more I thought about it, the more I decided I might merely have mistaken the approach of a shy local person at the ruins for something far more sinister. I didn't entirely believe this explanation myself but gradually my pulse approached something like normal when I regained the safety of the beach.

Rudy and Gabriela waved to me from the deck of the returning boat. They were both dripping wet from their underwater adventures and Gabriela's face was wreathed in a smile. I plopped myself down on the soft white sand and settled in, keeping a watchful eye on my surroundings while I waited for them to dock.

The boat pulled alongside a long wooden pier stretching out from the beach nearby and her passengers disembarked and headed for shore.

"*¡Hola, K.C.!*" Gabriela hailed me with a cheerful grin. "How was your walk? Did you have a good time?"

"Um..." I started but she raced on, gushing with the pleasure of her experience.

"We saw lots of funny colored fish and coral and Rudy touched a manta ray!" I cocked an interested eye at him, briefly distracted from my worries.

"What was it like?" I asked curiously and Rudy gave me an odd smile.

"Sort of rubbery, actually."

"Weren't you scared it was a stingray?" I added and

Rudy cast me an infinitely superior look.

"Manta rays are totally different from stingrays," he informed me, "if you know what to look for."

"Huh," I nodded, storing this for future reference.

"What did you do while we were gone?" Gabriela asked me cheerfully. "Did you visit the stores?" She meant the vendors lining the walkway near the restaurants behind us but I shook my head.

"Nope. I visited the ruins." Something about my reply caught Rudy's attention. He sometimes has an uncanny ability to sense what I am feeling.

"What's wrong?" Rudy asked. "Are you all right?" I licked dry lips and nodded, then shook my head.

"Yeah, I guess. But I think someone was following me back there in the ruins. "

"Following you? Are you sure?" Rudy asked me with a frown.

"I can't prove it, if that's what you mean. Whoever it was disappeared when some other people showed up." He was eyeing me doubtfully and I knew what he was about to say. "Yes, I know I might have been mistaken, because of everything that's been happening lately," I admitted reluctantly, "but I don't think so. There really *was* someone there."

"But it probably wasn't anyone following you, K.C. You've been pretty jumpy lately," Rudy remarked, relieved by this obvious explanation and he raised his eyebrows at Gabriela playfully. "Don't worry Gabriela, it's all right. K.C. just gets like this sometimes. Ever since she was a kid and I dropped her on her head she's been a little…shall we say…strange." Here he made a twirling motion with his forefinger near his temple and for lack of the right words to protest his unfounded accusation I splashed him, kicking the crest of an incoming wave all over him.

"Hey! Stop it!" Rudy spluttered in protest, even though he was still wet from snorkeling. "Cut that out!" He splashed me back then Gabriela splashed him and a water fight broke out. It was every person for him or herself after that, and by the time we left the beach everything we owned was dripping wet, even Father's camera, Fortunately it was of the water-proof variety, so no harm was done.

We took the next public bus back to Puerto Vallarta and arrived at the hotel as shadows were growing long on the streets. Father wasn't back from his meeting yet and I knew he wanted to go with me when I filed my report with the police so Rudy, Gabriela and I hung out in the lobby waiting for him.

Rudy and Gabriela settled side by side into the long wicker couch and proceeded to get into a discussion about the pros and cons of female bands on MTV. Gabriela told him the names of her favorite bands and they commiserated on the music of the lovely and talented, but late, *tejana* singer Selena. Meanwhile, I kept a wary eye out for suspicious-looking characters.

A van pulled up outside the hotel and its driver got out and headed for the lobby where we sat. He was wearing white pants and shirt and carried a large manila envelope. He approached the front desk and consulted briefly with the receptionist. I was surprised when she leaned over and waved Rudy over to the front desk.

"*¿Señor Flanagan?*" Rudy got up and crossed the lobby to them.

"Yes?"

"Señor, this has arrived for your father. It requires your, *¿como se dice en inglés?* Your signature." She pushed the envelope forward as well as the receipt Rudy was to sign. He did so with a flourish, tipped the delivery man then returned to his seat, putting the envelope on the table between us.

I'm a little embarrassed to say that the envelope sat there on the table beside me, right under my nose for another two full minutes or so before I finally happened to look at it and actually read the return address of the sender. And when I did so, it was out of nothing more than idle curiosity.

"Oh, Good Lord!" I exclaimed, clutching the envelope numbly. The words *'Sanchez y Sanchez'* were printed there quite clearly on the return address label and I gaped at the envelope in astonishment, blinking to be sure that my eyes weren't playing tricks on me.

"What's up?" Rudy looked away from the TV screen where four girls were performing a dance tune and likewise Gabriela tore her gaze from the screen to lift a querying eyebrow at me.

"This." I lowered my voice and spoke in a whisper, "It's for Father." I handed him the envelope and he studied it with a puzzled frown.

"So what?" he asked me finally, handing it back. "It's just an envelope, K.C. Nothing to be afraid of." It was obvious from his tone that he was humoring me and then I realized that I'd never told anyone the name of the law firm into which I had followed Rodriguez.

"The law firm that sent this envelope to Father," I pointed to the return address, "is the same firm I saw Rodriguez go into the day I followed him." Rudy took the envelope from me again and studied it.

"Sanchez y Sanchez." He read the label aloud thoughtfully. "K.C. are you *positive* about this?" I sighed.

"Yes, I'm *positive* it's the same firm," I replied, trying to keep my impatience from my voice. Just for once I wished he'd simply take me at my word. Rudy was silent for a moment.

"Just because it's the same firm doesn't necessarily

mean that what Father is doing is connected with this Rodriguez character," he said finally, "and remember, we still can't be sure the man you saw was even the same man as this Casteñada guy." I stared at him in frustration. Maybe *he* wasn't sure, but I certainly knew what I had seen. "But anyway we'll have to tell Father," Rudy finished firmly and I nodded, swallowing my annoyance.

"I know."

"Tell me what?" Father was standing behind us and at the sound of his voice I jumped nearly a foot into the air. "What's wrong?" Father asked, correctly interpreting our grim expressions.

"This." I held the manila envelope out to Father and he studied it with the same baffled look Rudy had worn earlier.

"I forgot to tell you the name of the law firm I followed Rodriguez to. It's the same as this one." I tapped the return address on the envelope.

"¿*Sanchez y Sanchez?*" He read the name of the firm aloud. "That's the firm that's handling the competing offer on the property. They offered to buy out our interest and sent over this proposal for me to take a look at." Father paced slowly across the lobby to stand directly in front of the television, blocking the screen where a trio of young men were doing interesting things with a chain saw and two guitars.

"These are very serious allegations," Father said soberly. "You're sure you've made no mistake about this?"

I snapped back crossly, "Why does everyone always ask me that? Of course I'm sure. I wouldn't say so if I wasn't."

"Maybe it has to do with the fact that you're always imagining things," Rudy muttered but I ignored him.

"I think it's time we all go and have a talk with the police about this. You too, Gabriela, if you have time." Gabriela gulped and looked at him.

"But I must take the bus back home or my father will worry," she murmured doubtfully.

"I'll call your father and tell him where you'll be, then we'll send you home in a taxi," Father assured her. "I think it's important that we go to the authorities about this right away."

"Don't be afraid Gabriela, you'll be all right," Rudy told her comfortingly and I eyed him resentfully as he seated himself in the back of the rental car with my friend, monopolizing her company and leaving me in the front seat with Father.

CHAPTER EIGHT

We drove downtown along a street called Morelos to where all the nightclubs were, lined up along a white concrete boardwalk called the Malecón. I saw Planet Hollywood, the Hard Rock Café, Carlos O'Brian's pub and a host of other happening nightspots which were already quite crowded even though the sun hadn't set. I thought it was a little early for a party but a sign in front of one nightclub advertised a 1 p.m. start of Happy Hour, which went a long way toward explaining the festivities.

"Won't the police station be closed?" I asked Father, looking around at the brightly dressed people celebrating the evening. I'd heard that some of the liveliest places in town stayed open until 5 a.m. but knew without even asking Father that he would never let me find it out for myself.

"This afternoon I called and spoke with an Officer García to make an appointment," Father replied quietly, concentrating on his driving.

We had reached the *Plaza De Armas,* or central plaza, as it was so fittingly named, at one end of the Malecón. Across from the plaza was the *Los Arcos* amphitheater, a large sculpture of three arches done in some kind of smooth white rock. I remembered the wave-carved huge rocks off Mismaloya beach and decided I knew how these arches had come by their name.

Close by the arches was an enchanting bronze statue of

a dolphin, fluid in the sunlight, and further back behind the arches I saw the scarred and pitted statue of what looked like a broken angel standing with his back to the sea. I turned to watch from the window of the car as a couple of tourists posed alongside the angel, grinning broadly while their companion took a photograph of them.

Puerto Vallarta's waterfront was filled with happy people out strolling along, catching the breeze off the bay. Perhaps it was the weather, or perhaps it was the glorious colors of the sunset, whatever the reason everyone seemed to be in a good mood.

I watched as an old woman selling paper flowers approached two young lovers walking along the Malecón. Shyly, the young man bought a pink paper rose for his sweetheart and put it in her hair while the old woman looked on, beaming like the sun. In the rear view mirror, I saw Rudy glance at Gabriela to see if she had noticed but she was looking out the other side of the car at a line of three dune buggies speeding along on the road beside us.

Brightly painted in oranges, limes and yellows, the buggies were piloted by bronzed, glowing tourist types who were evidently returning from a long day of racing along the open beach. They swept past us in a fast moving line, heading for the hills north of town.

It was easy to see that there were a lot of cool things for people to do in Puerto Vallarta. People who hadn't witnessed a murder, that is. I remembered our mission to the police station then and leaned back in my seat, feeling slightly sorry for myself as I watched the black, wrought iron street lights twinkling on to illuminate the evening.

A troupe of dancers was assembling near a restaurant which opened out onto the street and as we drove past, one woman stepped forward, leading the rest into a spirited and colorful display of swirling skirts and smiling faces. Just one of the sights I would have loved to see if I hadn't been on my way to give my report to the police.

"This is the nearest parking space. We'll have to walk the rest of the way." Father turned down a side street and parked along the curb, easing the dented rental car into a spot there. From there it was two blocks down the street toward a long, low white stucco building with barred windows. Two men in white uniforms were standing at ease near the door but as we approached they snapped to attention, one of them addressing Father politely,

"*¿Si, Señor?*"

"I have an appointment to speak with Officer García." Father told him. "My name is Flanagan."

"*Si, Señor Flanagan*. Will you please come this way." He led the four of us through the door and into a large waiting room, where he requested us to please be seated. We settled ourselves onto a row of plastic chairs there and waited.

Not far away a young man in a white uniform was typing something carefully into a computer. The clicking of his keyboard was the loudest noise in the whole room and looking around, I noticed that we were the only people waiting. No one spoke, and then the sound of footsteps echoing down a long, tiled corridor came plainly to our ears.

"*¿Señor Flanagan?*" A man dressed entirely in white, except for the gold and black badge sewn onto the sleeve of his upper arm, joined us with a smile and a handshake. "I am Officer García. Thank you for waiting."

"Thank you for agreeing to see us at such a late hour," Father answered warmly. "I wouldn't have bothered you but there have been a few strange things happening to K.C. that I thought she ought to tell you about." This was the under-statement of the year but I didn't point that out.

"How are you, K.C.?" Officer García smiled at me sincerely. He had a kind face, with deep laugh lines etched into the tanned skin of his face and I smiled back at him.

"I'm all right, thanks." I had the feeling that it would be a huge relief to unburden myself to this man.

"Let's all go back to the conference room," Officer García invited us all, "we'll be able to talk there. I will have your words typed up and you will sign them to make a formal statement, all right, K.C.?" I nodded again and we all followed him down a white tiled hallway to the conference room.

The conference room was exactly that, a large room with a big table surrounded by chairs. As a matter of fact it looked more like something from the public library at home than a place where interrogations took place. There was a pitcher of ice water on a wooden stand near the door and several glasses. There were more than enough chairs for the five of us plus the transcriptionist and we took seats more or less in a row, facing Officer García. Once we were all seated he began with me.

"Tell me what has been happening to you," he said and so I did. Starting with how I had witnessed Casteñada's murder, I told him about how I had followed Rodriguez to the law firm of Sanchez and Sanchez, and then how I had tricked the receptionist into giving me his name.

"You did that?" Officer García interrupted my narrative, a small smile hovering around his mustached mouth and I nodded. "Instead of just asking her what his name was?" García enquired and I shook my head at him.

"That wouldn't necessarily work. You see she might have been suspicious if a total stranger just walked in and demanded to know his name. Then she might have refused to tell me. The way I did it, she just automatically told me. Besides," I added defensively, "I didn't do anything wrong.

All I did was give him a free wallet."

"Yes. I see. Well." Officer García hid his smile and requested that I continue with my story. I told him about how I had met Gabriela and how we had recognized Casteñada in the newspaper as the man whom Rodriguez had killed. I told about how I had nearly been hit by a drunk driver, and lastly but not leastly I related the story of how I had recognized Rodriguez with the heavy-set man in the suit at Chico's Paradise, and felt myself followed in the ruins that afternoon.

"You were followed? Are you sure?" At the mention of the toad-like man Officer García's interest suddenly picked up.

"Well, no," I had to admit. "I've been sort of nervous lately. I might have imagined it." Officer García gave me an enigmatic but reassuring smile.

"I understand. Now, K.C., I'm going to need to ask you some questions, but they are strictly routine. I just need to verify some aspects of your story."

"All right," I told him, "ask away." Officer García proceeded to do so, posing a long series of questions and taking me back over and over again the events I had witnessed.

"It's for the record," he told me apologetically. "We need to get these facts on paper for future reference."

"What will happen after this report is filed?" I asked him after he had finished questioning me and I was signing the typed version of my story. "Are you going to investigate Rodriguez?"

"We will certainly ask him some questions about his relationship with Señor Casteñada and about when he saw him last," Officer García assured me dryly as he got to his feet. "Investigations sometimes lead nowhere here. But thank you for taking the trouble to give us this information," he told us all, his eyes on me. "I hope that the rest of your stay in Puerto

Vallarta will be very happy and safe from now on." "Thanks for listening," I told him sincerely. "Some people wouldn't have even believed me." I glanced sideways at Rudy as I spoke. "I will call you when we know more," Officer García assured us. "In the meantime, try to be careful. Don't go out unless it is necessary and avoid contact with people you don't know. In Mexico, sometimes people are not what they seem to be at first. Our policemen even get frustrated with this. We know that bad people can be, as you say, 'protected' by fallen angels." He was directing these instructions mainly my way, but his remarks seemed rather oblique.

"Don't worry, I'll be keeping an eye on K.C.," Father promised him as we left the police station.

While we had been filing our report with the police darkness had fallen over the city, and the lights had come on, colorful and dazzling under the myriad stars of the tropical night. Father hailed a yellow and white city cab for Gabriela and helped her in carefully, handing the driver several large bills.

"Muchas gracias." She turned to me. "K.C., I will call you in the morning, we will talk then." There was a serious glint in her eye and I nodded back, equally seriously.

"Good." The two of us still had a lot of things to discuss, things which were better said away from Rudy's inquisitive ear as far as I was concerned. We said goodbye after that and Father, Rudy and I watched as Gabriela's taxi disappeared into the night, becoming just another of many bright city lights in the distance.

"Can we stop in at the Hard Rock Cafe on the way back?" Rudy put in hopefully as we reached our rental car. "We do have to eat, after all." Father smiled a little at these words but shook his head.

"I don't think so, kids. I'm sorry to disappoint you but

I think tonight would be a good chance for us all to stay in and just take it easy. I have some documents to review and to be honest I'm beginning to think that things are getting a little too complicated for us here. No sense in us going out and borrowing trouble." Rudy scowled and slumped down in the front seat of the car.

"Thanks a lot, Kook Case," he muttered over his shoulder at me. "This is all your fault."

"It is not my fault!" I protested, not for the first time. "I'm not the one who killed Casteñada, Rodriguez is, so don't blame me!"

"Huh." Rudy snorted inelegantly at my defense but shut up and we drove home in silence after that.

I was blind to the attractions of Puerto Vallarta's nightlife. We drove past half a dozen places featuring live bands and dancing and all I could think about was getting to the safety of my room. I mean, the whole thing was really starting to give me the creeps. I had expected to feel better after talking to the police but now to my surprise I felt even worse than before.

I mean, up until then the whole situation had had a slightly abstract flavor, like something in a book or a movie. Having Officer García, an actual member of the police force, listen to my story and take me seriously had taken things from the realm of possible fantasy to cold, hard, reality and I have to admit I was feeling scared, especially with his last warning.

Suddenly I saw my recent brushes with danger in a far more serious context. It now seemed entirely possible that there was indeed someone after me, someone whose intentions were not good. From all indications that someone was either Rodriguez or the man who had been with him when he had killed Casteñada. And was the toad-man the real crime boss? I shivered, thinking about it. The more I pondered Officer

García's obscure reference to how investigations sometimes went nowhere in Mexico, the more I began to wonder if there was someone in the local government interfering with this case. Could it be possible that Rodriguez and Ravalos had friends in high places, friends who were protecting them from the police?

Beyond the obvious reasons the killers would have for wanting the only witness to their crime out of commission, I couldn't help wondering what else it was that they had to hide. I mean, besides the fact that they had murdered Casteñada, there was the unanswered question of *why* they had killed him. There had to be something more to the story that I hadn't found out yet.

"Do you know who employed *Sanchez y Sanchez* to make that competing offer on the property in Bucerías?" I asked Father as he parked in front of the hotel. He shook his head.

"No. They're handling it for an undisclosed buyer."

"Oh." I still couldn't see how it all tied in. "Maybe Rodriguez and his buddy are the ones behind the offer." I was only thinking aloud, trying to figure things out but Father swiveled in the driver's seat of the car to fix me with a piercing stare.

"K.C., this is entirely out of your hands now, do you understand me? Your part in all of this is over. I want you to do your best to stay out of trouble for the next few days, all right?" He was using his 'don't-even-think-about-arguing-with-me' tone and I knew better than to say another word. I simply nodded. "Do you promise?" He insisted, looking me squarely in the eyes.

"I promise I'll do my best to stay out of trouble," I told him sincerely, neglecting to verbalize my hope that trouble didn't come looking for me, either.

"Good. Because I don't want you out there trying to solve this thing on your own, K.C. That's a job best handled by the police at this point. Now, who's for take-out?" Father shifted gears abruptly in that way adults have when they are trying to distract you from something unpleasant. After a brief argument over what we wanted to eat (which I let Rudy win so he wouldn't throw a total fit) we had dinner delivered to our hotel room from a Chinese take-out place several blocks away.

We split up after eating. Father warned both Rudy and I not to set foot outside the hotel without first telling someone where we would be, and not to even think of venturing out at all after dark. Since it was already dark, we found that our evening entertainment options were limited to either Mexican folk dancing lessons in the ballroom, or what looked like some variation of bingo at the bar, which held little interest for either of us.

As you might imagine, Rudy was none too anxious for my company and so we opted for some private time alone in our rooms. When I was by myself I went downstairs to borrow a copy of the battered local phone directory for Bucerías from Carlos, the guy at the front desk. Carlos clearly considered my request an odd one but fished up the phone book anyway.

I took the stairs back up to my room two at a time and sprawled across my bed, flipping through the directory to see what I could find. The yellow section of the book contained several pages of advertisements for construction companies and I was able to find Señor Ravalos' company listed there with the rest.

'Ravalos Construction and Shipping' the ad said, and went on to list three phone numbers and an address. I jotted the numbers and addresses down in my notebook and continued my search, turning to the white section of the book.

I had little expectation of actually finding Ravalos'

name in the private listings as I figured him for the type of executive-style guy who'd have an unlisted number. I was right too, but fortunately Señor Angel Rodriguez was listed there, plain as day, along with about fifteen other Rodriguez families. I sighed and laboriously copied the addresses into my notebook. I was just finishing up when Father knocked at the door and came in.

"Oh hello, Father." I looked up as he entered my room, hoping he wouldn't notice that I had just kicked a phone book under my bed.

I didn't feel that I had disobeyed the actual spirit of Father's instructions to me, since I had obediently been keeping myself out of trouble by having an innocent read in the privacy of my own room. On the other hand, there was the slightest possibility that Father might interpret things differently if he knew I'd just been snooping for facts about *Señores* Ravalos and Rodriguez.

"Everything all right, kiddo?" he asked, his eyes softening as I smiled brightly back at him.

"Fine. Just fine." I continued to smile at him and we regarded each other thus for an instant.

"Well K.C., you know that Rudy and I are next door, so don't hesitate to call us if you need anything."

"I won't," I assured him, nodding and smiling.

"Sweet dreams," he said and left me alone. The only even remotely risky thing I did after that was to sneak down to the front desk to return the phone directory to Carlos. Then I went back upstairs and went right to sleep.

CHAPTER NINE

Father got called to another early meeting the next morning. "I want you both to stick together from now on, and keep each other informed if you leave your rooms, even if it's just to go to the front desk. If you do have to go out of the hotel, you're to go together. Is that clear?" Rudy and I exchanged mutinous glances then nodded silently. "Good." Father was in a noticeably grim mood. I attributed it to the stress of his assignment compounded by recent events.

"I'm planning to do some checking on your theory about the connection between *Sanchez y Sanchez* and Rodriguez today," he told me, "So I'd appreciate it if you would both try and stay out of trouble until I get back for lunch. Fair enough?" We nodded at him again and after making sure we had the number of his pager Father left us to our own devices.

"So, what do you want to do?" Rudy asked me then, more than a trifle irritable about having to include me in his plans for the day.

"I thought I'd go check out the Municipal Market," I suggested. "Want to go?"

"What's that?" Rudy asked, his interest piqued.

"The guidebook calls it a flea market," I informed him.

"Well," Rudy's eyes narrowed as he considered my suggestion, "I guess it wouldn't be all that bad. But after we go there we have to go to the beach," he added, sending me a warning look.

"All right," I agreed with a careless shrug and having reached a workable compromise we headed out into the city together.

I walked along behind Rudy as we headed along Ignacio Vallarta toward the market, which is located on the other side of the *Rio Cuale*. Neither Rudy nor I were really following our instructions to stay close to each other. I simply wasn't as interested in stopping to talk to every pretty girl selling beaded necklaces and bracelets as Rudy clearly was, and he didn't care one way or the other if we ever reached the Municipal Market. Once or twice I was forced to wait impatiently for him while he chatted and flirted and schmoozed. When I spotted the market ahead of us I confess I didn't wait for him but headed across the bridge toward it alone, knowing that Rudy would catch up to me in a little while.

I was crossing the actual bridge itself, relaxing in the sunshine, when I heard rapid footsteps behind me. Someone dropped a heavy hand on my shoulder, and I turned impatiently, expecting to see Rudy there. Instead, I found myself face to face with Rodriguez.

I was frozen for a split second, the time it took me to double check my first reaction and recognize him. Up close I could see that he had smallish eyes deeply set into a blocky brow. His skin was pocked and tan and his lips narrow, unsmiling. His right hand was buried in his pocket and it looked like he held something bulky there, something like maybe a gun.

I didn't wait to find out what it was, though. Reacting quickly, I wrenched myself out of his grasp and looked desperately around me for an escape route. The bridge stretched ahead of me, looking like the first one hundred yards of a track and field event and that's exactly how I treated it.

Sprinting north along the sidewalk I took the stairs three

at a time from the bridge down to the island below, hoping to lose Rodriguez among the profusion of trees there. He shouted something at me and then I heard the pounding of his footsteps following me. The chase was on.

I reached the bottom of the stairs and kept running, past a colorful cluster of vendors selling Mexican handicrafts from stalls. Any other time and I would have stopped to admire them but I could hear the sound of leather shoes slapping the tiled walkway behind me, proof of the fact that Rodriguez was still following, so I kept running.

I made a split-second decision to double back around behind a thatched hut where a girl was advertising day cruises. For a moment I hoped I'd lost Rodriguez but then I heard him behind me again, cursing rudely in Spanish when he discovered my trick. There was a small group of people clustered around a juice vendor's stall, watching as she deftly squeezed fresh fruit into colorful glasses for them. I screamed and shouted, "Help!" as loudly as I could while running toward them. Naturally they turned to stare at me but unfortunately, by the time they realized the situation my pursuer and I were past, running away from them. Nor did I see any of the friendly white uniformed policemen who usually patrolled the area so conspicuously.

To my left a wood and rope suspension bridge stretched out across the river, with two giggling teenage girls clinging to the braided handrail as the bridge shifted and swayed under their feet.

"Gangway!" I shouted as I pounded out onto the bridge. The boards were solid enough beneath me but they were supported only by ropes which started to stretch and twist like an angry slinky-toy when my weight hit them. The entire bridge swung perilously to the right and then back to the left as I did my best to continue running across it. The teenage girls ahead of me turned to look at me, expressions of amazement on their faces as I ran past.

Just as I reached the end of the bridge I felt it tighten under the weight of my pursuer and I glanced behind me at his face. Rodriguez shouted something fiercely at me, his face contorted with a mixture of rage and deadly intent as he hurried across the bridge. I couldn't help shuddering, he didn't even seem winded yet and boy oh boy did he ever look mad!

His anger was abruptly replaced by frustration and rage when his feet slipped out from under him and he fell, sending shock waves up and down the length of the bridge. His mishap caused the teenage girls to burst into giggles again, clutching at each other and at the sides of the bridge to support themselves in their mirth as he staggered to his feet.

I turned to survey the street before me at a glance. To my left the street continued straight towards the city. Ahead, likewise. No cover there. I looked right and saw my salvation, the Municipal Market itself. The *Mercado Municipal* was huge, its red-tiled roof extending over an interior which appeared to be home to hundreds of individual vendors selling silver, beaded jewelry, embroidered shirts and hats.

I ran inside fast and kept on running right past three silver vendors, then turned right in front of the lady selling embroidered scarves, sprinted past two stalls full of straw dolls and then I took a left by the saddle salesman. I paused and doubled back around a nearby mask stall to end up crouching behind a pottery vendor's wares. Anxiously I waited, my heart pounding in my chest.

There was no sign of Rodriguez. Either he had lost my trail or he had decided that there would be no point in following me through such a crowded public place. Either way I eventually felt safe enough to stand up and smile at the pottery vendor who had been watching me with mild perplexion.

"Gracias," I said and bowed a little. He grinned at me toothlessly, his face creasing into sharp lines of amusement as he bowed back.

I headed through the rest of the market building until I came out on the far east side. The front of the Municipal Market opened onto a bridge not unlike the one I had taken to reach the west end of the island and for a moment I felt a sense of disorientation until I remembered that there were two bridges over this island.

I crossed the bridge quickly, heading south. I felt very exposed walking along like that when at any moment I might encounter my pursuer again and so I kept looking for him in every face in the crowd, hoping to spot him before he could spot me. I saw no trace of Rudy, nor did I feel inclined to retrace my steps and go looking for him.

Thinking it might be best to lie low for a while and see if Rodriguez was still following me, I found a gate opening onto steps leading to the river and walked cautiously down.

The flat tiled stairs were cool beneath my feet and I found a white iron bench by the water where I sat down, watching the entranceway warily as I waited. A large white heron strutted through the shallow water, basking in the shade.

The utter tranquility of the place had an other-worldly quality which contrasted sharply with my recent brush with danger and I started to shiver, taking stock of my situation. There was no way that Rodriguez had just wanted to talk to me. I felt sure that he had intended to silence me, one way or another, on the subject of Casteñada's untimely demise. Close on the heels of that unlovely thought I realized that the longer I waited quietly the more opportunity I was giving Rodriguez to find me, if he were still looking.

I knew I couldn't stay there any longer so I left the riverside, tiptoeing back up the smooth tile steps to the brightness of the street. Pausing for a moment under the pretext of admiring the red flowered tulipan trees along the river I looked around for Rodriguez, my heart pounding in great sickening thuds at the mere possibility of encountering him again.

There was no sign of him but I was in no mood to take any chances on being recognized. I paused at a street vendor's stall ten feet away long enough to buy a bright blue cap which I donned after leaving my straw hat behind on a window sill.

I walked with the cap pulled low over my face to yet another vendor's stall where I bought a bright blue long-sleeved beach shirt with the words Puerto Vallarta written in huge and blocky letters across the front of it. This I pulled on over my own blouse. It was hot but served as an effective disguise since it changed my appearance entirely.

I headed briskly for the hotel, keeping my head down while darting nervous glances around myself. Despite my near certainty that I had lost Rodriguez I was aware that he could pop into sight at any moment and the thought made me hurry. I reached the safety of the Hotel Fontana Del Mar without ever seeing any sign of Rodriguez but I did get quite a few interested stares from the people I passed on my way back.

"Where have you been?" Rudy demanded angrily, when I joined him back at the hotel lobby. "You just disappeared back there!" His expression changed from irritated to bemused disbelief. "That's what you bought? *That's* what we went all the way across town for?" He asked, his tone heavy with sarcasm.

Glancing down at myself I noticed that I was still wearing the beach shirt I'd bought for my disguise earlier. I hadn't really noticed it before but in addition to the words 'Puerto Vallarta' printed in green block letters across the front of the shirt was the slogan, *'¡Una cerveza, por favor!'* It was the Spanish equivalent of 'gimme a beer, please!' and below the words was a picture of a pink, smiling man quaffing a huge mug of the stuff, half of which had dribbled down the front of his shirt.

"Aren't you a little young to drink?" Rudy asked doubtfully, looking at the shirt, "Or were you maybe planning to give it to Father?"

"I didn't really notice what it said," I told him. "Listen Rudy, I —"

"You didn't notice what a shirt you were buying looked like?" He repeated dubiously and I scowled at him. "What's *up* with you, Kook Case?"

"The shirt isn't important," I told him impatiently. "Listen Rudy, Rodriguez tried to grab me on the bridge back there. That's why we were separated. He chased me all over the island and I only lost him at the market."

"Rodriguez did? Are you sure?"

"Of course I'm sure! Quit asking me if I'm sure! I wouldn't say so if I wasn't." I snapped at him sourly, fear making me rather cranky. It's not every day that I escape from known killers and I must say the experience had not improved my mood at all. "Look, Rudy. I think I'd better just stay here in the hotel until Father gets back. This thing is getting way out of hand." Rudy regarded me soberly but didn't challenge my choice.

"I guess that would be a good idea," he agreed, scowling a little at the loss of an afternoon on the beach. "And I'll stay here with you, to keep you safe," he offered. Macho man, as though Father hadn't ordered us to stick together. I made use of my downtime by calling Gabriela, who answered on the third ring.

"*Buenos dias.*"

"*Hola,* Gabriela, it's me, K.C. Listen, Rodriguez just

tried to grab me." I got right to the point.

"He did?" She sounded thoughtful, rather than dubious.

"He sure did, he even chased me around some but I outran him." Just remembering it made me scared all over again and I sat down hard on the chair near the desk in my room as my legs turned all rubbery on me.

"Are you all right?"

"Yes. I mean no. I don't know. I guess I'm just pretty freaked out right now is all." There was a short silence, then Gabriela said,

"I have been talking with my father, who has been asking questions around town. He says that Señor Rodriguez is involved in many bad things, him and the man he works for, Señor Ravalos. There are many rumors about the things he does but my father won't tell me what. When I asked he became angry and told me I should stay away from him. Señor Rodriguez, I mean." There was a pause then she continued. "K.C. I have to talk to you about this but not here, on the phone. Nose to nose."

"You mean face to face," I corrected. "All right. Can you come here? I can't leave the hotel right now, it's not safe."

"Then I will go there," she said firmly. "We have to talk. I have been asking questions of my own and I found out some things."

"Well," I hesitated, thinking it over. "All right. But I think you should be careful too. I mean, Rodriguez isn't after you, he's after me because I'm the one who can connect him with the Casteñada murder, but who knows what he'll do next? Personally I think he's nuts."

"Nuts?" Gabriela was confused.

"I mean, crazy. Loco. Off his rocker." There was a brief pause as she tried to decipher my obscure reference to furniture and I put in, "Um, never mind about the words, just be really careful, O.K.?" Gabriela seemed to consider my warning then she agreed.

"All right, K.C. I'll be there in an hour." We hung up and I headed next door to Rudy's room. He answered at my knock with a booming "come in."

Rudy was sitting at the desk in the room he shared with Father, writing postcards. He glanced up and smiled, apparently having temporarily forgotten that I was the reason for his forced confinement. "Oh, it's you." I took the seat across from him and positioned myself so that I had a clear view of the street below. I didn't really have a reason for dropping in on Rudy. The truth of it was I had nothing to do until Gabriela showed up so when he asked again,

"So what's up?" I just shrugged.

"Just hanging out, I guess. Gabriela's on her way here." Rudy's eyes crinkled in an approving, if slightly lecherous smile.

"Good," he observed. "She's cool."

"Yeah." I nodded and we relapsed into comfortable silence as Rudy finished the card he'd been writing.

After a full hour of watching a program about the wonders of the coral reef I glanced at my watch and then rolled over to check it against Rudy's small travel alarm on the bedside table. Almost an hour and a half had passed since I'd spoken to Gabriela and there was no sign of her.

I paced to the window and looked down the street toward the direction from which she would be coming. Any minute now, I told myself. Half an hour later I was still pacing back and forth across Rudy's room while he watched an excellent Mexican soccer team do their stuff and tried to ignore me.

Thirty minutes after that, I started to really worry. At

first I tried to ignore the sense of deep unease which crept over me, telling myself that perhaps Gabriela had just gotten a late start or something. After twenty more minutes had passed, I called Gabriela's house. When her mother answered it she assured me that Gabriela had left over two hours ago and I felt my stomach turn into a ball of ice.

"All right then, she's probably still on her way." I tried to speak naturally. "Tell you what. Why don't I have her call you when she gets here so you know she's all right?" Gabriela's mother agreed that this was a good plan and we hung up.

"What's up?" Rudy turned the sound off and watched the game on mute while waiting for my reply.

"Something's happened to Gabriela," I told him flatly. The aura of impending doom which had been hanging over me for the last few days seemed to have condensed into a certainty that my friend had met with trouble.

"Yeah?" I had Rudy's full attention now. "Like what?" I shook my head.

"I don't know. Maybe what almost happened to me today," I replied grimly. "All I know is she was supposed to be here already." I checked my watch, "She left two and a half hours ago, the trip takes an hour, she's an hour and a half late." Rudy's eyes widened and he sat up straight, the soccer game forgotten. For once he didn't argue with my logic.

He nodded slowly. "She would have called if she could have."

"An hour and a half is more than enough time to find a phone and tell someone you're going to be late," I agreed.

"What should we do?" Rudy asked me, as though I had a plan. I started to shrug but then I stopped to think it over. Even without any proof I knew that Gabriela's disappearance had something to do with all of the freaky stuff that had been happening lately.

"I'm thinking that Gabriela is still in Bucerías," I replied thoughtfully. "I mean, consider this. It all leads there. The whole dispute over the vacant property, not to mention the fact that Rodriguez and Casteñada are from there, the law firm, everyone involved has something to do with that town, even us," Rudy was watching me with a hint of impatience so I wound up quickly, "all things considered, if someone interfered with her, it's likely that it happened in Bucerías." Rudy swallowed and cleared his throat dryly.

"Interfered with her?"

"Interfered with as in clobbered her over the head, ran her down in a car or kidnapped her," I clarified, drawing on recent history to support my case. Rudy nodded slowly and paced over to stand next to me by the window where I was still technically keeping watch for Gabriela.

"We'd better call the police right now," Rudy decided.

"There isn't time," I shook my head. "We have to go there and help her, if she's still..." I couldn't bring myself to say the word aloud but we both heard it loud and clear anyway. "If she's all right we need to find her as quickly as possible before they have a chance to do anything to her," I finished hastily.

"How would we know where to look?" Rudy asked doubtfully.

"We know the addresses of two of the people involved," I told him.

"We do?" Rudy wrinkled his brow at me. "And how do we know that?"

"They were in the phone book." Then I told him, "Listen, all that isn't important right now. She needs help!" Rudy nodded, reaching for the phone.

"And that's why we're calling the police. They have

those cars, you know?" He was giving me his 'wise older brother' look. "They also have guns and badges and they can turn on their sirens and break the speed limit and stop people. You know?" Here he opened his eyes extra wide at me to make his point. "They get to do do all sorts of things that ordinary civilians just can't do." I knew what he was saying but I still disagreed.

"They're also the ones who ask you to come downtown, check your identity, ask you to fill out papers and then tell you they'll have the next available officer on the case. After which they waste time making sure you aren't just some lunatic with an over-active imagination and by the time they believe you it's too late!" I wasn't being entirely fair to Officer García and the Mexican police but I was trying to make a point.

"Father told us to stay here," Rudy reminded me grimly and I ground my teeth. I knew that too, of course, but I still believed that if Father had a chance to objectively evaluate the situation he would agree that sometimes rules were made to be broken. Surely he would see that, in this case, an exception had to be made. After all, Gabriela's life might depend on it.

"There is absolutely no way you're going there alone," Rudy told me quite sternly. "And I know I'm not going with you so you might as well sit down and relax while I call the police." I recognized that we had come to an impasse. I also recognized that Rudy meant business. I shrugged.

"Go ahead then. Call the police." I nodded at the phone. "The number's right there by the keypad." I watched as he picked up the phone and dialed. A short conversation ensued and he was put on hold.

"Yes. This is Rudy Flanagan speaking. Flanagan. I'm calling on a matter of some urgency," He began, and paused, turning to look at me quizzically. "K.C.? What was the name of the officer from yesterday?"

"Officer García," I replied.

"May I speak with Officer García?" Rudy asked and there was another pause while the call was transferred to a different division. "Yes, I will hold."

"I'll be right back." I headed for the door.

"K.C., hang on...what? Oh, yes. *Sí, Señor.* Please put me through to Officer García. *Muchas gracias.* Oh...I see. Well, then can I speak to his assistant?" I tiptoed out of the room as Rudy was explaining to Officer García's assistant what his call was about.

I knew I had to move fast, before Rudy got off the phone in time to stop me. I raided my room for the rest of my money and left the hotel at a run.

CHAPTER TEN

I got into the first taxi I saw on the street and when the driver looked at me quuestioningly I told him, "Bucerías."

"Bucerías?" He stared at me disbelievingly over his shoulder but when I nodded he shrugged and started the taxi.

"Three hundred pesos," he added and when I agreed he swung the taxi into traffic.

"¿*Señorita* is a tourist?" he asked as we swept past the Malecón north toward Mexico 200 and I nodded. "You go to see the bullfight?" I shook my head. "You like the cockfight?" He persisted and when I shook my head again he lapsed into silence until we reached the city limits.

While I wouldn't say that he did a better job of driving to Bucerías, the taxi driver certainly went a lot *faster* than Father had, passing other cars recklessly and facing oncoming traffic with the misplaced bravado of a matador.

"You like Mexico?" He grinned at me in the rear view mirror as we swept by a VW beetle moving along sedately at the maximum speed limit of 60 kilometers an hour.

"I like Mexico, yes." His driving made me totally nervous but since speed was so exactly what I wanted I refrained from making any critical remarks.

"Why you go to Bucerías? For sightseeing?" he asked and I nodded, unwilling to distract him from the road with any kind of lengthy explanation.

"Yes."

"Bucerías is very pretty," he informed me. "You like to swim?"

"Yes," I answered again.

"Nice beaches there. You can find many things in Bucerías. Music, dance, party." I had different plans entirely but I didn't think it would be a good time to explain. "You like to party?" he continued slyly, his grin intimating that he for one certainly liked a good party, as should everyone. "*Norteamericanos*, they like to party," he remarked. "You know?"

"I like to have fun." I shrugged.

"I have a friend he can get you the party," the taxi driver told me. I stared at him, puzzled and trying to decide if this remark really required a reply. "You know?" He waggled his brows expressively at me. "You like?"

"I don't think so." I shook my head, uncertain as to exactly what he was advertising. Only one thing was for sure, I knew I wanted no part of his party.

"Many people in Bucerías, they like to party too." He went on cheerfully, "If you like I introduce you to my friend."

"I already have a friend," I replied, meaning Gabriela.

"You know someone?" he asked, clearly surprised. I nodded.

"I'm going to see her now."

"My friend give you better price," he assured me with a wink.

"Price?" I was utterly confused. "For what?" He misunderstood the nature of my question.

"For smoke." He made an inhaling gesture with two fingers and I thought he was asking for my permission to light up so I shrugged, resigning myself to tobacco fumes.

"Please do."

"Me?" Now he was confused.

"It's all right," I told him, "It's your taxi." I didn't
care one way or the other if he smoked, the windows were
halfway open and I could always open them farther if the smoke
got too bad.

"You want smoke now?" He gave me an odd look of
approval which I couldn't quite fathom and I shook my head.

"Not me, you!" He didn't seem to be following me so
I explained, "The only way I'll ever smoke is if I catch on fire.
But you feel free to go ahead."

"Catch on fire?" He was lost as we reached the outskirts
of Bucerías and I told him to pull over near the spot where
we'd parked a few days before. He shook his head dubiously
but accepted three hundred twenty pesos for the ride, tip
included, as I got out of the taxi.

"My friend, he has the best smoke in town," he
informed me, revving the engine with a shrug. "Better than
your friend's. I sell you for fifty pesos." To my astonishment
he glanced furtively around then reached into his front shirt
pocket. "You try?" He held out a strangely wrapped cigarette
and for the first time I realized that we had been talking about
two completely different things.

"Oh." I backed away. "No. Thanks. No thanks." He
shrugged, waved at me cheerfully and pulled away in a cloud
of dust as I mentally kicked myself for being so dense. Drugs
aren't a major part of my world but still, I'd seen enough to
know what they were and to realize that I'd just been offered
an 'Acapulco golden' opportunity.

I trudged along the road toward Gabriela's house
intending to see if anyone there had heard from her but then I
changed my mind and decided to use the phone instead. I
wouldn't put it past Rudy to have called Gabriela's parents
when he discovered that I was missing, and to have told them
to stop me if I showed up. Sure enough this was the case.

"K.C.!" Gabriela's mother answered the phone. "Your brother Rudy, he called here to look for you."

"I know. I'll call him," I told her. "Say, has Gabriela called?" There was a pause and her mother answered, "We are out looking for her. My *esposo*, how do you say..."

"Husband," I put in.

"Yes, my husband has gone to find her." I nodded at the phone.

"Good. I have to go now but I'll keep in touch." I hung up before she could start asking me things like where I was, what I planned to do, you know all those things that take so much time to explain. Then I called Rudy.

"K.C., where the heck are you?" he demanded without preamble when I greeted him.

"Um, listen Rudy," I winced even before his reaction. "I'm in Bucerías. I have to look for Gabriela, you understand that, don't you?"

"I understand that you are in one heap of strouble," he assured me grimly. "I called Father from his meeting and he's on his way here." There wasn't much I could say about that and just then the thought of Father's wrath didn't help me concentrate on my mission to save Gabriela either so I saved that worry for later.

"Well, I'll be looking around Señor Rodriguez' place a little. If I don't find Gabriela there I'll try the Ravalos' construction site, all right? Tell the police when you call them where to come to look for me. I'll be in touch." I hung up before he could lecture me further.

I knew Father would be beyond angry with me, but I felt that I could live with his punishment more easily than I could with my own guilt if I didn't try to help Gabriela. And I had a feeling that with a little luck I *could* help her. Somehow.

The fact that I didn't have an actual plan bothered me somewhat but I couldn't make one until I knew where she was. So I began my search.

The first address listed under Ravalos Construction and Shipping proved to be a zero. There was little there, no people, no bulldozers or cranes, just two large sheds that graced the patch of arid land which matched the address in my hand. I stared at the underdeveloped lot curiously. There wasn't even an office of any kind on the site, as far as I could tell.

I walked around to check the place out anyway, just to be sure that Gabriela wasn't hidden there somewhere but I soon found out she was nowhere around. The only structure of any type even remotely suited for hiding a prisoner proved to belong to the neighboring address, a hardware store. I wondered where Ravalos' business office was then decided I must have written down the wrong address.

An old dog panted lazily at me from its small patch of shade under the porch of a nearby house. It sniffed in my direction then thumped its tail as though to suggest that it would forego the usual formalities and let me pass with no further inquiry. I stopped to pat it then went on.

It was early afternoon and the brutal tropical sun beat straight down on my shoulders. I walked away from my first investigation frustrated, hot and thirsty enough to need a drink, *muy rápido*. The main street in Bucerías wasn't very far and I quickly found a little store there selling film, water, juice, candy, gum, chips and other miscellaneous snack foods. I opted for a bottle full of cold, clear water and drank half of it off in one gulp while the man behind the counter studied me surreptitiously.

I left the store and settled down in the shade of a big palm tree to check my notebook for Angel Rodriguez' address. There was something maddeningly familiar about it, and after a moment I realized that I had recognized the address because it was directly adjacent to the vacant property that Father's company was bidding on and therefore the addresses were almost identical.

I put the notebook and map away and headed down the street toward the access side of the lot, remembering that it bordered on the Rodriguez house in a tangle of bush and trees. The paved road underfoot ended and I walked quietly along a dirt footpath toward the nearest side of Rodriguez' property to my position.

As I drew closer I recognized the white marble pillars and yellow stucco facade of the house I'd admired from the beach two days ago. With recognition came the realization that it had to be the Rodriguez house. It looked the same yet different somehow, now that I knew who it belonged to.

I edged carefully up to the brick wall surrounding the border and eyed the barbed wire dubiously. I'd never actually climbed over barbed wire and it didn't seem like fun but then I never got the chance to find out if it was or not because someone behind me spoke softly saying,

"Looking for something, *Señorita*?" I froze and in the ensuing silence I distinctly heard a metallic click, as though someone had just cocked a gun at me. I turned around ever so slowly, momentarily stunned by my predicament and recognized the man behind me as Rodriguez. Again.

"Hello." I swallowed hard, trying not to blink as his eyes bored into mine. "What are you doing here?" I've often heard that the best defense is a strong offense but in this case it didn't accomplish much.

"Me?" His face darkened. "No, *Señorita*, the question is, what are *you* doing here?"

"Oh, nothing. I got lost." I gestured weakly at the bushes stretching along the beach. "I was taking a walk on the beach." I tried to bluff things out but Rodriguez would have none of it.

"You've been snooping around my house," he accused me, "just like you snoop into everything."

"Well," I tried for a nonchalant shrug. "I guess I'll just be going now. Sorry if I disturbed you." I was planning to make a run for it but he stopped me by seizing my arm in a cruel grip.

"Shut up." Rodriguez was obviously tired of playing games. "And put your hands up, yes, where I can see them, and walk along the fence toward the house. That's it." He nudged me a little with the cool metal barrel of the gun.

Well, let me tell you, it didn't take a rocket scientist to figure out that I was in deep trouble. I did as he said in silence, moving cautiously so as not to startle him into doing anything foolish like shooting me. Not that there was any doubt in my mind that he would do so, eventually.

"Where's Gabriela?" I asked, surprised that my voice wasn't shaking as badly as the rest of my body was. "Did you kidnap her?"

"Be quiet," he snapped at me and I shut up, walking in silence as he pushed me toward a gate which provided us entrance to the immaculate grounds surrounding his house. He shoved me toward a door around the back of the house and I paused, not wanting to leave the sunlight for the unknown darkness of the interior of the house.

"Go inside," Rodriguez ordered me curtly. When I still hesitated he wrenched the door open and gave me a push which sent me sprawling. "Inside," he repeated as I got slowly to my feet, watching him apprehensively. I found myself in the kitchen of his house.

Gleaming steel and white tile, equipped with every convenience known to man (or woman as the case was more likely to be), the kitchen was huge. We followed a long airy hallway from the kitchen down to an even wider hallway which led to a large room, one entire wall of which was composed of picture windows overlooking the sea. Rodriguez gestured roughly with the gun at a chair near a small desk and I sat down.

"So," he addressed me, "you are the nosy little brat who gets involved with things that don't concern her. You could have had your nice quiet vacation in Puerto Vallarta but no, you had to interfere, didn't you?" He seemed to wait for my reply, even though it seemed like more of a rhetorical question to me.

"Well," I said finally since he was still looking at me, waiting for an answer, "if you didn't want someone to see you then why did you and your buddy go and kill Señor Casteñada right out in plain view like that?" I was only answering his question but he took offense at my words, his finger tightening ever so slightly on the trigger. I held up a hand, as if to stop the bullet and my voice quavered as I continued,

"It won't do you any good to shoot me, you know." I could only hope to talk him out of what he planned to do. "I already told the police all about you and Señor Ravalos." I was bluffing, presenting my theory as though it were fact.

"What do you know of Ravalos?" Rodriguez asked me so irritably that I knew I had struck a nerve.

"I know that you work for him, that you two killed Señor Casteñada, and that you probably have pretty heavy protection from some important person in government. That much is obvious." I had his attention, and as he listened to my words he lowered the gun slightly. I took this as a good sign and redoubled my efforts to keep him talking rather than shooting. "I still don't see why you would kill Casteñada in the first place. Was it something to do with drugs?" His eyes flickered, betraying his reaction to my words and I knew that my guess was close to the mark. Unfortunately he also raised the gun again.

"What does that matter to you, you little meddler? Soon there will be no witnesses and therefore no more investigation." Rodriguez was eyeing me with malicious satisfaction and I knew he was right. Without me around to testify as a witness to Casteñada's killing there wouldn't be any case against him, and Rodriguez would get away with the murder. He pointed the gun straight at my head, eyeing me along the length of the barrel.

"So I kill you now. Say goodbye, *señorita*." Time stood still, I had a second to mentally apologize to Father and Rudy then there was a low laugh from Rodriguez who lowered his gun and sneered at me. "Feeling brave now? Feeling smart?" I swallowed hard, more afraid than I had ever been in my life. I stared at him wordlessly as he slid the gun into an inside pocket of his jacket.

My whole body turned to jelly then and I was glad I was sitting down. I'd never been so terrified in my entire life, never. I'd really thought he was going to shoot me and I was forced to acknowledge that it maybe hadn't been such a good idea after all to go chasing after Gabriela. For the first time I found myself sincerely wishing I'd taken Father's advice about staying out of trouble.

"Stay there and don't move," Rodriguez told me, crossing the room away from me. I'd seen Rodriguez in action before and I knew he'd pull the trigger with no regrets and even fewer reasons so I did as he instructed, sitting motionless on the chair.

He reached for the phone and punched a number while keeping a watchful eye on me. Someone answered the phone at the other end and Rodriguez began to speak rapidly. I did my best to translate.

"It's me. Yeah. Say, listen, I have some news. That girl from Vallarta, she's here with me now. She was snooping around my house. What should I do with her?" Rodriguez' eyes narrowed as he listened to the reply and for the first time ever I saw him smile. It was not a pretty sight, nor did I find it at all reassuring. "She's (something) we can do (something) at once." After sharing a sinister chuckle with the other person on the line he hung up and looked at me. I looked back, trying not to let my fear show while I waited for him to make the first move.

"You little (something)," he muttered under his breath. "We are not finished, *Señorita*. Ravalos wants to talk to you, but when he is finished with you he has promised me I can kill you." He assured me of this most contemptuously, as though taking my life would be no more to him than swatting a fly would be. I gulped.

"Now move." He directed me up out of the chair back down the hallway again and out the back to the carport behind the house. There were three cars there, a jeep, no doubt for Rodriguez' early morning jaunts on the beach, a pickup truck with the words Ravalos Construction and Shipping in Spanish on the side, and a dark sedan. He shoved me into the sedan's front seat, and motioning me over to the passenger's side, climbed in after me.

I sat quietly in the front seat beside Rodriguez as he pulled out and headed back toward the highway. He had his gun in his lap right where he could use it if necessary and I knew there was little I could do to extricate myself without at least being shot.

I thought about making a break for it anyway but when I tried the door handle surreptitiously I found it locked by a master control only he could reach. No escape there. I would have to wait until we got out of the car to make my move.

Rodriguez turned right onto a street which sloped sharply upward and shifted into a lower gear as we followed an avenue running up to the crest of the ridge. We were climbing. All around were houses and people, in cars, on foot and bikes, but there was no way I could call for help. I had never felt quite so alone in the middle of a crowd.

We left the residential part of town and took a broader, paved road leading to a small stand of trees at the tip of the ridge. I could see the ocean from this point and wondered where he was taking me. It crossed my mind that he was bringing me to a cliff, perhaps to push me off.

We passed the stand of trees at the end of the ridge and turned off the road to go through massive iron gates linked by a long, high wall of brick evidently surrounding someone's estate. Rodriguez guided the car down a driveway leading down along the curve of the hill and turned off, stopping the car. There before us was the coolest house I'd ever seen.

Wrapped around the flank of the hillside, the house was made of white stucco with a red tiled roof. There were balconies on all three floors. Since the top of the hill was level with the top of the house I could see that there was a helicopter landing pad at one end, over what looked like a garage below.

Giant palm trees shaded this veritable oasis and a fountain sparkled and gurgled down several levels of the hillside past the house to end up in a crystal blue swimming pool surrounded by palm trees and thick green grass.

I could see the somewhat distant figure of a man lounging poolside. Without speaking, Rodriguez hauled me out of the car and jerked my arm painfully, forcing me to walk down the stone stairway leading toward the pool. I took the steps slowly, looking around for possible avenues of escape.

CHAPTER ELEVEN

M ove." Rodriguez gave me another shove when I got to
the bottom of the stairs and I hesitated, looking at the
man sunning himself by the pool twenty feet away.

"Oh, hello." As if just noticing us for the first time,
the man stirred and turned to watch our approach. He wore a
white silk shirt and white linen slacks, very elegant. "How
nice of you to join us, Miss...?" His tone was heavily ironic
so I took his words at face value and introduced myself.

"Flanagan. Konstantina, to you."

He smiled. "Konstantina. What a lovely name, Greek
isn't it? I am Antonio Carlos Ravalos." Señor Ravalos was a
gorgeous man, thick dark eyebrows arched over eyes which
were an astonishing hazel in color. When he smiled at me he
looked better than a movie star. I watched him carefully,
painfully aware of Rodriguez' fingers embedded in my upper
arm.

"¿Mi amor?" A woman's voice, high, light and incon-
gruously sweet interrupted our introductions. I tore my eyes
away from Ravalos' handsome face and looked across the pool
to where a young woman was sunbathing, topless on a vividly
patterned lounge chair. "Who is that with you?" She sat up,
shading her eyes as she looked toward where Rodriguez,
Ravalos and I were. Tanned and perfectly formed, she had
short hair so blonde it was nearly white. She paused to pick
up a silk robe flung carelessly over the back of her chair and

wrapped it around herself then stood, belting it about her waist as she strolled toward us.

"Ahh, Maribel, my love," Ravalos gave her a smile and waved to her without rising, "come meet Konstantina." She crossed to his side and sat on the edge of the pool at his feet, stretching out her hand to me as though we were at a party. Nonplussed, I shook it. Up close I could see that her features were as perfect as Ravalos' were, she had a pouty mouth, small nose and eyes so startlingly blue they looked unreal as she gave me a puzzled look.

"Konstantina? Isn't that an instrument?" she asked innocently. "My brother used to play the Konstantina when we were in high school." I opened my mouth to reply then closed it again, totally at a loss for words. "Are you here sightseeing?" She continued, obviously trying to be nice. I glanced at Ravalos uncertainly and he directed his words to Maribel, speaking slowly as though she were a child.

"She's here because Rodriguez found her snooping around his house," he told her patiently. "She's the one who's been causing us so many problems." Maribel's eyes widened and her lips formed an 'O' of surprise as she released my hand hastily. I noticed that she, too, had perfectly white teeth.

"Really." She stared at me as though I were an unknown species of something she'd just found crawling in her soup. "But she's just a little girl," she pointed out. Ravalos shrugged.

"A very nosy little girl. But we'll still have to deal with her."

"Oh well," Maribel stood and stretched, languid as a cat, "whatever." Apparently losing all interest in matters of life and death she stooped to give Ravalos a kiss on the cheek. "You work too hard, darling." She told him and with this remark turned and strolled back to her lounge chair by the pool, shedding her robe as she stretched out in the sun again with a sigh of sheer contentment.

"Now." Ravalos turned to smile at me, his sensual lips curving over even white teeth. "Where were we?" He looked so charming that I almost felt a moment of doubt that he could be the brutal figure behind what had been happening in Bucerías.

"You were about to consider letting me go," I suggested hopefully. After all, it wasn't as if I had anything to lose by trying. At least, so I thought until Rodriguez tightened his grip on my arm, his fingers biting clean down to the bone and I winced despite myself.

"That's enough, Lorenzo, no marks on her, not yet." Ravalos' smile never wavered. "Please, take a seat, *Miss* Konstantina."

"If it's all the same to you I'd rather sta—" I never finished the word because Rodriguez' hands came down on my shoulders with a thump which forced me to my knees half on and half off the chair. "Thanks." I whispered as I seated myself.

"That's better." Ravalos was close enough for me to smell the musky aftershave he'd chosen that morning. "Now, *Miss* Konstantina. My friend and associate Mr. Rodriguez tells me that you have been messing into my business." He stared right into my eyes and I felt the chill of them clean through me. "Why have you chosen to make trouble for me?" Suddenly his extreme good looks seemed no more than a misleading facade for the danger that lurked beneath.

"Um," I considered my options and decided that, as bad as things were they could still get worse. "I'm sorry." I tried to smile apologetically at him but my lips were too dry to even stretch past my teeth. "Believe me I'd much rather be on the beach." He was not amused by my attempt at humor and I stopped trying to smile.

It was time for me to bluff so I did my best to appear cool, calm and collected while ignoring a sudden urge to vomit from sheer terror. "Look, Mr. Ravalos, killing me won't do you any good. I've already filed a report with the police. If you kill me now you'll just make everything worse for yourself."

"Is that so?" He leaned closer, his nostrils thinning as he continued to smile and I looked away, doing my best not to recoil. "And what did you tell the police? Did you make up stories about bad men doing bad things that scared you?" He was taunting me, smiling mockingly at my averted face and even though I've heard ten times worse than that from my beloved brother Rudy believe me, this was totally different. Really nasty, in fact. I cleared my throat.

"I told them that you were the man with Rodriguez when Casteñada was killed." I lied. "I also called them about an hour ago so they'll be here any minute now." I had no way of knowing for sure that Ravalos had actually been the man with Rodriguez that night but my deduction was proven correct by Ravalos' reaction. His eyes flickered ever so slightly and he glanced away at Rodriguez then back at me.

"But when they come you will be dead and there will be no proof that what you say is true. Anyway, our friends will make sure the investigation goes nowhere." Ravalos leaned back in his chair, crossing one leg over the other, looking suddenly gorgeous again and even though I was scared I felt a brief flash of resentment that he could dismiss my life so easily. It suddenly occurred to me that I really didn't want to die. At the same time I also had to admit that the way things were looking, I surely would.

"That's true." I looked Ravalos right in the eyes, trying not to let him see my fear. "The police have no evidence at all, really. None except for the footage from my video camera." I shrugged and looked away. He arched an eyebrow at me in query,

"Footage?"

I nodded, trying to feign unconcern.

"You know, the video film I took of Rodriguez and you beating Casteñada to a pulp." I admit I was improvising freely about the video footage, but hopefully he had no way of knowing that. "And I got a nice clear shot of you and Rodriguez carrying Casteñada out to the car after you killed him, believe me." I could only hope I sounded convincing enough to make him think there would be no point at all to killing me.

"Film?" Ravalos' mouth turned down in a scowl as he got to his feet. For a moment I thought I'd pushed him too far and braced myself. "You made a movie of us?" Ravalos glared at Rodriguez who was shifting uncomfortably from foot to foot then suddenly stood and whirled on him. "You idiot! I thought you said it was safe!" He raged and I felt a moment's reprieve as Ravalos shifted his anger to Rodriguez.

"I didn't know she had a camera. How could I know she would be watching?" Rodriguez replied sullenly. He made no attempt to disguise his anger at being accused. "Besides, you were the one who said we should kill him there in the hotel room, remember? You finished him off!" Ravalos stalked over to where Rodriguez stood and slapped him hard across the face.

"You shouldn't have been such a fool!" Ravalos' polite veneer had entirely eroded away and I saw the true ugliness under his good looks as he attacked his partner in crime. Across the pool Maribel watched us with detached interest, sipping at a frosted drink by her side.

"How was I to know she would be watching?" Rodriguez repeated. A dull red flush crept up from his collar and he balled his hands into fists rather than strike back at his boss. "It was all your idea anyway!" Rodriguez protested further, his eyes glittering strangely in the sunlight. "Enough!" Ravalos slapped him again. "You disappoint me, my friend!" He sneered and turned his back on Rodriguez to pace over to where I still sat, motionless. Maribel lost interest in our little drama and rolled over on her stomach, settling in comfortably while far away a bird sang its heart out, the melody at odds with what was happening before me. I kept my eyes fixed on Ravalos.

"And you say the police are coming here?" he asked me, suddenly as smooth as silk again and I nodded, frightened by the way his eyes burned into mine.

"They'll be here any minute," I bluffed, praying that Rudy would have called them and passed on my message. Ravalos eyed me thoughtfully for a moment then turned back to Rodriguez who was rubbing a hand slowly along his jaw where Ravalos had just struck him twice.

"I don't believe you," he announced suddenly. "You are bluffing." It was no more than the truth but I just kept my mouth shut, knowing better than to deny his accusation. Ravalos seemed to reach a decision. "Take her downstairs. Lock her up with the other one, we'll deal with them later." He instructed Rodriguez and Rodriguez nodded, apparently forgetting the insult to his pride.

I knew he meant that they would kill me later but I felt the sudden birth of hope at his mention of the 'other one'. The other one they were referring to had to be Gabriela, and if they hadn't 'taken care' of her yet perhaps there might still be a chance for both of us.

Rodriguez seized my arm and shoved me in an elbow-twisting, painful way back along the pathway leading up to the house. He pushed me hard every few feet, making it difficult for me to keep my balance and although I tried to move quickly that didn't stop him from shoving me some more. I got the impression he was enjoying his assignment to the max.

We reached the top of the hill and walked around the side of the house to what looked like a garage combined with a loading dock behind it. The loading area was much larger than anything I'd ever seen in a private residence and I had to wonder whether Ravalos personally conducted his business from his house.

I paused to look at a red Mercedes parked in the garage next to a Ravalos Construction and Shipping truck. Rodriguez gave me a violent push toward the garage section, indicating that I should take the stairs that led upward on one side of the room.

"Move," he snarled, and bullied me along a short hallway to a door at the end. Taking a key ring from his pocket, he unlocked the door. "Inside," he told me curtly and without waiting for me to comply he seized my shoulder in a bone-bruising grip and flung me in, slamming and locking the door behind me. I caught a glimpse of Gabriela's surprised face as I bounced off the wall and toppled over onto the floor.

"Hi, Gabriela." I sat up and brushed the hair from my eyes, shakily.

"K.C.!" Gabriela scrambled over to help me. "Are you all right? Why are you here?"

"I was looking for you at Rodriguez' place and he caught me," I told her. "How about you, are you all right?" Gabriela nodded and forced a smile.

"I'm fine. A little scared."

"Yeah, I see why. Me too," I added unnecessarily. "What happened, how did you get here?" Gabriela grew a shade paler.

"I was on my way to the bus stop when Rodriguez stopped his car and pulled me inside. He said he'd shoot me if I didn't get in. He had a gun so I went with him," she finished.

I couldn't help looking around the room as we talked. Gabriela and I were in a small concrete cell lit by a single unshaded bulb overhead. The faint smell of mildew from a mop in a bucket nearby wafted to my nose. There were no windows and only one door, and judging by its furnishings it seemed obvious that the room was a mop closet.

"So what's going on here?" I asked Gabriela, listening nervously for the sound of approaching footsteps as I stooped to examine the door which barred our escape. "Why did they kidnap you?"

"I found out what's going on," Gabriela told me, her voice lowered to a whisper. "Señor Ravalos is the smuggler!"

"Smuggler?" I looked at her sharply and she nodded. "What does he smuggle?" I asked and Gabriela's face fell.

"I don't know. I think it might be guns or something," she replied thoughtfully. I frowned at the door. The hinges were smooth stainless steel, built right into the door so I wouldn't be able to take it off its hinges to effect our escape. So much for Plan A.

"Maybe it's drugs," I suggested, studying the small utility shelf over the door. There was nothing there except a bottle of bleach and a short length of clothesline along with a few dirty rags. For a brief instant I wondered if Maribel did the housework for Ravalos then discarded the notion on the grounds that it was far too ridiculous to even entertain.

"Drugs?" Gabriela repeated and I nodded.

"A guy tried to sell me some marijuana right here in Bucerías," I informed her, thinking of the taxi driver. Gabriela frowned, considering it. "Maybe they killed Casteñada because he found out that Ravalos is smuggling marijuana." I finished.

"What are we going to do?" Gabriela looked terrified. "They will kill us too."

"Not if we can stop them they won't," I assured her fervently.

"How can we stop them?" she asked, puzzled but interested.

"The way I see it, it's like this. Ravalos wants us dead but he probably won't do his own killing; he'll send Rodriguez. That means Rodriguez will be the one we have to deal with, right?" I checked to see if she had been following my logic and Gabriela nodded thoughtfully, a faint glimmer of hope in her eyes.

"Yes."

"So when he comes in here to kill us there will be two of us and only one of him. That gives us an advantage." I tried to speak convincingly, hoping my words would prove true. "We'll have to jump on him and get his gun," I finished. Even to my own ears the plan seemed more than a little underdeveloped.

"How can we jump on him? You mean, we bang on the door and when he comes we hit him?" Gabriela asked.

"No not like that," I told her, "because if we bang on the door he'll know something is wrong and he'll be ready for trouble. We have to surprise him."

"How?" Gabriela asked again and I frowned. It was a good question.

"One of us has to get up on that shelf over the door and when he comes in to get us, drop down on him. Then the other one of us hits him with the mop." I waved at the shelf I was referring to and Gabriela considered it.

"It's a good plan," she admitted, adding doubtfully,

"but will the shelf hold?" I shrugged my shoulders, unsure. "Only one way to find out. Help me up." Gabriela locked her hands together and I used them as a step. She heaved me up with all her might and I was able to get an arm and a leg over the edge of the shelf. It creaked a little but held under my weight. I climbed onto it and stretched myself full length along it like a cat on a window sill.

"Now what?" Gabriela asked and I shrugged, very carefully.

"Now we wait." And wait we did. It seemed like hours went by, although in reality it was only about half an hour later when we heard footsteps outside the door.

CHAPTER TWELVE

R eady?" I whispered to Gabriela, and she nodded, standing
in the middle of the room, holding the mop in her hands
like a batter at the plate. She looked terrified. I know I was.

I had little doubt that Rodriguez would use his gun if
he had to and the success of our plan hinged upon whether the
two of us could take him by surprise. The footsteps approaching the door to our prison cell were purposeful and, when I
heard the key turning in the lock I readied myself, leaning
perilously over the edge of the shelf as I waited.

Rodriguez entered the room, stopping just below me
as the door closed and locked behind him. I could tell from
Gabriela's expression and the way she was watching something
he held out of my sight that his gun was aimed at her.

"Where's the other one?" he asked sharply, glancing
around the room for me but before she could reply I launched
myself from the shelf above directly onto his shoulders,
landing with as much of an impact as I could manage from a
distance of about a foot over his head.

Rodriguez staggered and went down, cursing rapidly
in Spanish while I hung onto his gun arm with all my might.
Gabriela bashed him with the mop, aiming for his head and
shoulders and making contact with every blow. Eventually his
grip on the gun loosened. I seized it and rolled away.

"Freeze!" I whispered loudly, lying on the floor and
pointing the gun right at him. "Leave her alone!" Rodriguez

had managed to get to his knees and was in the process of yanking the mop away from Gabriela but at the sound of my words he turned slowly towards me, raising his fist.

"You can't shoot me, little girl, the gun isn't even loaded," he told me contemptuously, starting to get to his feet. "Isn't it?" I hefted the weapon. "Let's see." I pointed the gun right at his head, using both hands to steady my trembling arms and he froze, an extremely worried expression crossing his face. Sometimes it pays to be a bluffer, for as a bluffer myself I recognized his words for the empty threat that they were. The gun was loaded.

"Get back down on the floor," I told him flatly and he must have known that I meant what I said for he dropped his arm and glared at the two of us, speechless with rage as he lowered himself down onto the dirty grey tiles. I stood up and backed away, keeping the gun pointed straight at him.

"Get the clothesline," I told Gabriela. She eased around Rodriguez, reaching for the roll of nylon cord. "Tie him up, hands first, then legs." I kept the gun aimed at Rodriguez and when she had finished I handed it over to her and added a few knots of my own. I'd never really thought my nautical training would amount to much on dry land but as it turns out, a good knot can be useful on many occasions.

When we were finished, we had used the entire length of clothesline and Rodriguez lay rolled and tied up on the floor like an old carpet. I nodded in approval. His arms were bound so tightly to his sides that he could hardly move his fingers and his legs were wound around with about ten feet of rope.

We didn't have anything else to gag him with except the dirty rags on the shelf so we used those, stuffing them deeply into his mouth as he choked and swore at us, saying things in Spanish which made Gabriela wince. It was a relief to finally silence him.

"There." I smiled at Gabriela, dusted my hands off and pocketed the gun very carefully as she smiled back. I was glad to see that the terrified expression had fled from her face, as it must no doubt have left mine. I hadn't totally thought our risky scheme would work but it had and we seemed to have an actual chance at escape. Gingerly reaching for the key ring in Rodriguez' pocket I unlocked the door to our prison cell.

"Bye." I smiled at him over my shoulder as we left, taking a measure of enjoyment at the helpless anger I saw in his eyes as he watched us go. Then the door closed and locked.

"Which way?" Gabriela breathed into my ear. The long empty hallway leading back to the garage stretched before us.

"I do not know the way out. Rodriguez blindfolded me when he brought me here. Did he blindfold you too?"

"No," I answered. It occurred to me that the reason he had felt no need for this precaution was because he had been planning to kill me for sure but I pushed this alarming thought away, preferring to look on the bright side.

"Let's get out of here," I whispered back., "This way." I intended to lead us back the way I had come in and into the trees surrounding the house where we could take cover from any search party following us. It might be awhile before Ravalos came to look for Rodriguez, or it might be only a minute. Our best hope was to make the most of our chance at escape while we could. We crept back down the hallway to the garage.

I was heading for the open garage door leading to safety when something stopped me. Something told me that the key to our current trouble was somewhere nearby. I couldn't explain how I knew this but I did.

"What are you doing?" Gabriela whispered furiously as I skirted the red Mercedes and approached the truck parked beside it.

"I just want to check on something. It'll only take a second," I whispered back, holding up a finger to shush her. Gabriela rolled her eyes impatiently at me but waited while I looked the truck over.

It was big, white and boxy, the kind of truck you might see on the road every day without really noticing it, with all the normal signs of wear and tear. It was loaded with several wooden crates, neatly stacked against one side. I couldn't help wondering just what was inside those crates.

"This'll only take a second," I whispered to Gabriela and climbed up into the bed of the truck, trying to make as little noise as possible. I was aware of the urgency of our predicament and the need to flee, but for the life of me I couldn't resist having a peek inside one of the crates.

There was no sign of anyone else in the area other than ourselves, but I kept a watchful eye on the doors as I lifted the lid off one of the crates. To my disappointment it contained nothing more than what looked like building materials. Stainless steel pipes, plumbing materials and other rather ordinary tools of the trade.

"What is it?" Gabriela had followed me warily and stood beside me in the truck bed, looking at the contents of the crate.

"I don't know. Looks like building materials," I replied, trying not to sound as baffled as I felt. I reached for one of the pipes and lifted it cautiously. It seemed unusually light and I studied it more closely. The pipe itself was hollow, of course, but more than that, the metal forming the pipe itself was hollow too. I felt a flicker of excitement as I examined it and found that one end unscrewed, like a cap.

"*¡Madre de dios!*" Gabriela exclaimed in a whisper as I poured a fine white powder from the pipe onto the floor. "It looks like cocaine!"

"So that's what this is all about." I scooped up and wrapped some of the powder in a twist of packing paper which I put in my pocket, then I replaced the pipe, satisfied with the results of my search. "O.K., let's go." Gabriela nodded and we headed for the driveway leading to the woods behind Ravalos' house.

There was no sign of pursuit. Apparently Ravalos had not yet missed his buddy Rodriguez and the alarm hadn't been raised. Gabriela and I edged along the outside of the garage, peering carefully around the corner as we reached the end closest to the trees. I could see the pool below us and there was no sign of either Maribel or Ravalos, evidently both inside the house.

"On the count of three we make a run for it, to those trees," I whispered and pointed. Gabriela licked her lips and nodded. "One...two...three...go!" We sprinted together for the safety of the trees and I was excruciatingly aware that anyone looking from the picture windows above us would have a clear view of our flight.

We reached the shelter of the trees and huddled close to the ground, panting. I was mentally plotting our next move when suddenly Gabriela seized my arm in a grip almost as painful as Rodriguez' had been.

"Ouch! What?!" I pulled my arm free, following her gaze to stare at a car parked in front of the house. "What's the matter?" I whispered. "Come on, let's get out of here!" Gabriela shook her head, sadly.

"It is my father's car," she whispered. "We have to stay and help him."

"He must be there looking for you," I suggested. We huddled behind a large, flat leafed bush to discuss our next step. The sharp report of a gunshot silenced this whispered discussion and Gabriela and I froze, gaping at each other as the echoes from the shot died away.

"Oh, no," I said, at a loss for other words.

"He has shot my father," Gabriela said, with a certainty I felt myself. "We must go back." Now, let me tell you the last thing I wanted to do was return to Ravalos' lair, but it wasn't like we could just leave after that. We had to do something to help Señor Velazquez. I bit my lip.

"All right, let's go back," I whispered. We approached the house at a run, zigzagging from bush to bush. It struck me as odd that there was no one on the premises to see or stop us. I would have thought Ravalos would be the type to employ a ton of security personnel but apparently he wasn't. Either that or his staff was on an extended lunch break somewhere.

We saw no one at all until we were well inside the garage and then to my alarm there was the sound of approaching cars from the driveway behind us. It was easy to figure out that they were headed for the garage and to where we were standing, right out in plain sight. We looked at each other in consternation.

"Now what?" Gabriela breathed, her eyes wide with panic.

"Over here." I sprinted towards a floor-to-ceiling utility cabinet built into one side of the garage, not far from where the truck was parked.

"In there?" Gabriela protested at my choice but didn't stop to argue since the approaching vehicles were close enough for us to hear the men inside them talking. We scrambled inside the cabinet and I pulled it almost closed, leaving a crack to see from just as the first of two more Ravalos Construction and Shipping trucks pulled to a stop in front of us.

"Over there!" I heard a shouted instruction then the sound of a slamming door and a man strode into view. I could see him quite clearly but not who he was waving and talking to. "Just a little more. There, that's fine. Now let's make this quick, *amigos*. After this job is done we will all take a nice, long vacation. *¿Entienden?*"

There was a murmur of mingled laughter and assent then two more men crossed my line of sight, each pushing a hand cart piled high with more crates. All of them were wearing khaki pants and white shirts with the words Ravalos Construction and Shipping on them.

"Uh, oh," I muttered under my breath. Gabriela and I listened, trying not to make the slightest noise while some crates were packed onto the truck we had searched earlier. It soon became obvious that we were witnessing one of Ravalos' incoming shipments and I couldn't have imagined a worse place to be at that moment.

Despite the fact that they laughed and talked as they worked, creating a general air of jocularity, the men loading the crates all wore handguns and two of them even had what looked like semi-automatic rifles slung casually over their shoulders.

I had no doubt that they took their work very seriously. The cargo they were loading had to have been worth several million dollars and I felt certain that they would be highly motivated to protect it from intruders like us. Gabriela and I waited for what seemed like ages, listening until we heard the sound of slamming doors and of truck engines being started.

"*¡Vamos, amigos, one more load!*" I heard someone shout and then to my dismay, there was also a rattling, rolling sort of sound, as though someone had pulled the garage door down and then there was a clang and the sound of a bolt being slid home.

"Rats!" I swore, easing myself out of the utility cabinet. I tiptoed over to the garage door and gave it a yank, trying as hard as I could to pull it up, but of course it was locked on the outside. We had no choice but to try to escape through the house.

"Mi padre." Gabriela put a worried hand on my arm and I nodded, well aware that he might be facing worse danger than we were at the moment. I was opening my mouth to whisper that we still had the gun and could use it if we had to when we both heard the sound of approaching footsteps, followed by a man's voice.

"Rodriguez! Rodriguez, you idiot, where are you? We have another problem!" It was Ravalos and I winced as I realized that he was about to find out about our escape. Gabriela and I stared at each other. For once I was at a loss but she pulled my arm urgently, heading quickly toward the stairs leading down from the house before Ravalos appeared.

I spotted her destination right away and we sprinted as though trying out for the Olympic games, hiding under the stairs just as Ravalos reached them. His feet descended not two inches from our faces, and for a moment I toyed with the idea of reaching out to trip him but gave it up when I saw the gun in his hand.

Gabriela saw it too and her eyes widened. If Ravalos was holding the gun then for sure he must have been the one who had fired the shot we'd heard earlier. Since Señor Velazquez was in the house with him that meant that Ravalos had probably shot him. (Assuming, of course, that he hadn't shot Maribel.) My fears were somewhat allayed when Ravalos turned to gesture behind him at someone, saying,

"You, Velazquez, come down here."

"You will never get away with this!" I recognized Señor Velazquez' voice as he limped down the steps, one at a time. His right foot left a bloody track on the stairs and I saw Gabriela whiten as she noticed this. "I will not be the only one to come asking questions," Velazquez continued angrily.

"There has been much talk in Bucerías about you and your business." He said the last word contemptuously.

"There will be no one left to talk when I am finished," Ravalos sneered in return. "I will kill you and your precious daughter along with that pesky *norteamericana* tourist brat." Gabriela's jaw tightened as Ravalos strode down the hallway toward the door of the small mop closet and turned the handle, before realizing it was locked.

Ignoring Ravalos' threat, Señor Velazquez spat out, "Where are they, you (something) of a dog?!" Ravalos turned to sneer at him, fishing in his pocket for a key to the mop closet.

"Be silent, fool." Ravalos unlocked the door and entered the mop closet as Gabriela and I watched breathlessly. There was a muffled crash from the mop closet then the sound of Ravalos' voice cursing irritably in Spanish.

CHAPTER THIRTEEN

Y ou idiot! You have let them get away!" Ravalos was
shouting at Rodriguez. A moment later, he returned and
strode across to the utility cabinet, from which he took a long,
sharp-looking machete. "Don't move," he snarled at Velazquez, who was leaning against the wall near the stairs and
breathing heavily. I could see that he had been shot in the right
thigh and that he was having trouble staying upright but was
somehow managing it. It didn't look like he was capable of
standing much longer, let alone running away.

Ravalos entered the mop closet with the machete and
a moment later emerged, followed by a shame-faced Rodriguez, from whom freshly cut clothesline was still dangling.
It occurred to me that Gabriela and I should have taken our
chances on rescuing her father before Rodriguez was freed,
but it was too late for us to do anything about it and so we
waited.

I slid Rodriguez' gun carefully from my pocket and
held it in both hands hoping fervently that I would never have
to use it. I have been asking Father for two years to let me
attend gun safety training but he says I have to wait until I'm
sixteen, so I knew I would have to put my faith in luck rather
than skill to use it effectively.

"I cannot trust you to do anything!" Ravalos was livid
with rage as he faced Rodriguez. He was actually trembling
with anger and I noticed that his beautiful features were

downright repellent when he raged. "The little girls have escaped and it is all because of you!" Ravalos spat sideways on the ground. "You cannot even handle two little girls!"

"They jumped on me from above," Rodriguez shot back angrily, clearly humiliated to admit this defeat. "They took my gun."

A smile spread across Velazquez' face at these words and he put in, "The police will certainly catch you two fools." Both men ignored him.

"Maybe you are just getting careless." Ravalos' lips twisted into a caricature of a grin. "Or maybe you are just too stupid to follow my orders," he suggested softly and Rodriguez raised his head at this insult. He stared straight at Ravalos, clearly at the end of his patience.

"It wasn't my fault," he retorted through a clenched jaw. "This whole thing was your idea, remember? You were the one who said we should kidnap the local girl to keep her father here from going to the police. What good did that do? *Eh*?!" Rodriguez was shouting now, his face nearly purple with anger while Ravalos seemed, by contrast, to be suddenly made of ice.

"*You* were the one who planned this whole thing! You and your friend in the justice department." Rodriguez continued his rant: "You said we would double our business but you don't even have enough men for the job! So you force the fishermen to help us with our business. Now that was stupid, my friend! If it hadn't been for you, Casteñada would never have gone to the police in the first place and we wouldn't have had to kill him!" There was a long silence, broken only by the sound of the two men breathing heavily as they faced each other.

"You don't like the way I do things around here, is that it?" Ravalos' words were soft, almost placatory. "You think we need to change some things around here?" Rodriguez seemed to realize that he had gone too far and his eyes narrowed as he tried to regain control of his temper. "I think you always blame me for your mistakes," he replied evenly and the two men continued to watch each other. Rodriguez finally gave a little shrug and looked away. "I will find them both and bring them back," he promised, turning away, and then as though in slow motion I saw Ravalos raise his gun, pointing it right at Rodriguez.

"You already had your chance." Ravalos snapped and then pulled the trigger. The shot was deafening in the closed space and I watched in horror as Rodriguez slumped to the floor, a red stain spreading across the back of his shirt. It's a cliché, but it is really true: time can stand still, and a second can feel like a lifetime. Gabriela put a hand over her mouth to quell her own scream and I stepped out from under the stairs, facing Ravalos and pointing Rodriguez' gun at him.

"Drop that gun!" I told him loudly. "Right now!" Ravalos' smile faded and he half-turned to see me standing there. "Don't move!" I warned him and his triumphant expression changed to one of disgust.

"You!" he snarled, a combination of rage and disbelief on his face.

"Do it!" I barked, trying to sound like a cop in a movie and he dropped his gun to the floor where Gabriela retrieved it then crossed the hall to help her father. Velazquez limped painfully at her side. "Inside the house," I ordered Ravalos nervously, "and move very, very slowly. Don't even think about making any sudden moves," I warned him.

I made him lead us up the stairs and into the house while Gabriela followed, supporting her father. We walked past several spacious, exquisitely appointed rooms and I found my mood worsening. I always find it demoralizing to see how well the bad guys of the world live and Ravalos was no exception.

I mean who was the person who came up with the expression, 'crime doesn't pay'? Because in Ravalos' case it obviously had.

Behind a half-open door I spotted a jacuzzi, along with white marble fixtures and colorful mosaic tiles which must have cost a fortune adorning the room. I thought longingly of happier times and the day when this would all be over and I could relax with no worries. Someone was singing of love in an off-key soprano inside the bathroom and I barked,

"Come out of there with your hands up! Now!"

"Darling?" The singing stopped and Maribel's voice echoed plaintively through the tiled bathroom.

"Come out of there right now with your hands in the air!" I snapped, trying for a tone of unquestionable authority. "I have a gun and I'll use it!" There was a pause, then:

"Well you don't have to be so nasty," she remarked. "Just a moment." She emerged into the hallway before us, flushed and pink as though fresh from the shower. She wore a white terry cloth robe and pink, fluffy slippers on her feet. "What's going on?" She stopped and stared at the four of us, nonplussed. "Why do those little girls have guns?" Then, she added slowly, "Where's your gun?" Ravalos scowled at her and snapped:

"She has taken my gun from me, you fool. Can't you see that?" Maribel continued to watch us, wide eyed.

"Why did you let her do that?" She asked him with a frown. "I thought we were going to go away tonight." Ravalos muttered something under his breath and I sighed, gesturing at Maribel with the gun in my hand.

"You'd better come with us," I told her. "But be very quiet or else I'll shoot you." She studied me, her eyes wide.

"You won't shoot me," she told me matter-of-factly and although she was probably correct in her assumption I shrugged, trying for an air of hard-boiled cynicism.

"How can you be sure?" I asked her. Maribel considered it for a moment then sighed.

"Oh, all right. Just a minute." She disappeared back into the bathroom and emerged again, holding a fluffy white towel which she wrapped around her head, turban-style. "There. I'm ready." She followed Ravalos docilely as he led us the rest of the way into a large living room, with floor-to-ceiling picture windows on three sides overlooking the lawn and pool below.

There was a small grand piano near a leather couch in one corner of the room, a large-screen television in the opposite corner and several rows of mahogany bookcases almost entirely filled with lurid-looking paperback novels. A nearby mahogany credenza was cluttered with an assortment of beanie babies and I thought I recognized Maribel's homey touches in the decor.

Without waiting to be told, Maribel flounced across the room and plopped down on the leather couch there. Folding her arms across her chest and crossing one leg over the other she swung a pink-slippered foot back and forth, clearly impatient to get back to whatever she had been doing before we had so rudely interrupted her.

"Have a seat." I gestured to the couch with the gun, indicating that Ravalos should join her and when he still hesitated I added, "Move it." He snarled and spat in my direction viciously, apparently at a loss for words. The glob of spit landed near my foot on what must have been a priceless Persian carpet woven in rich hues of black, ruby red and blue-green.

"Antonio!" Maribel shrieked and clapped a hand over her mouth, her composure shaken by his action. "Don't ruin the carpet!" Ravalos flushed and shot her a withering stare.

"Sit down on the couch next to her," I ordered him, my confidence increasing in leaps and bounds now that we had control of the situation. "Gabriela, tie them up," I added.

"With what?" She asked me and I tore my eyes away from Ravalos for a second to look around.

"I don't know, how about the cord on those drapes over there?" Gabriela nodded and pulled the cord on the tapestry drapes so hard that the entire assembly came crashing down. Maribel whimpered and Ravalos cursed angrily under his breath but complied when I eyed him down the barrel of the gun.

"Be quiet," I told him. Gabriela tied his wrists tightly and used the leftover cord to tie Maribel's wrists to his so that they sat awkwardly bound together, back to back on the couch.

"You will be very sorry for this, little girl," Ravalos warned me, a small tic starting near his left eye. "No one does this to Antonio Carlos Ravalos. No one."

"Those drapes cost a fortune!" Maribel added reprovingly, then yelped, "Ouch! Antonio don't do that! It hurts!"

"Shut up, both of you," I retorted, then added, "Now where's the phone?" I was intending to call the police but I never got the chance.

"Not so fast, *señorita*." The words were spoken from behind me in a familiar voice and I froze, my new-found confidence leaving me in a rush. "Put the gun down." The voice instructed from behind me and Gabriela, who was looking over my shoulder at the speaker, obeyed and tossed the gun she'd taken from Ravalos onto the floor in front of him. She looked resigned, and I slowly turned to see what she was looking at.

Three men, the same ones we'd seen earlier, were standing there behind me, holding machine guns pointed straight at me. Believe me, I got that serious sinking feeling in the pit of my stomach again.

"You too, *señorita,* drop the gun," one of them advised me, and I dropped the gun near my foot where I could possibly retrieve it. "Now kick it away," he told me and I did so immediately. "All of you, go stand over there, very slowly." Gabriela put an arm under her father's shoulder and helped him limp over to sit near the piano where I joined them.

The man closest to them crossed the room and quickly cut the cord which bound Ravalos and Maribel. Ravalos stood up and eyed the three of us with a look of murderous rage.

"So the tables have turned." He strolled closer and sneered at me, rubbing his wrists savagely. "You are not so brave now, are you, little girl?" I swallowed hard, wishing myself elsewhere and wishing I hadn't been so insolent to him earlier.

"I have bruises now." Maribel eyed me resentfully, studying her arms with a pout. "Shoot her, Antonio."

"Señor Ravalos, Rodriguez has been shot!" the first man interrupted us impatiently, "We found him lying on the floor downstairs. It looks like he's finished. Dead!"

"Rodriguez dead? How?" Maribel's jaw dropped and she forgot her injuries with the shock of this news.

"That one did it," Ravalos told them, pointing right at me and the sheer outrageousness of his lie took my breath away. I gaped at him like a fish out of water while Gabriela defended me.

"That's a lie! K.C. did not shoot Rodriguez, you did, Señor Ravalos! We all three saw you do so!" An awkward pause followed her words and the three men eyed one another warily as Ravalos shrugged and smiled at them.

"Do you believe what she is telling you? I tell you, the *gringa* shot Rodriguez," he insisted smoothly.

"No, I didn't," I replied as calmly as I could, and

glancing from one to the other of his three men I addressed my words to them. "Ravalos is the one who shot Rodriguez. They got into a fight because Ravalos made a mistake and blamed Rodriguez for it."

"Silence!" Ravalos directed a stinging slap at me and I reeled back, ducking in time to miss the worst of the blow. What did connect was enough to stun me for a moment though, long enough for Ravalos to take charge again.

"Has the last shipment come in?" he asked the man nearest him.

"It is downstairs, being transferred. Juan and David are handling it," the man replied and I did a mental tally. Counting Ravalos and the three men in the room with us, that meant a total of six heavily armed men against two girls and a wounded man. I noted to myself that these were rather uneven odds. (I didn't include Maribel at all in my calculations.)

I glanced over to where Gabriela was still holding her father and was alarmed to see that Velazquez looked like he'd taken a turn for the worse, probably from blood loss. He seemed to be wavering in and out of consciousness. Gabriela gave me a desperate look and I spoke up loudly.

"You know what, Ravalos? Killing us now won't do you any good at all because I already called the police and they'll be here any minute." The three men with guns exchanged nervous glances and I pressed my slight advantage, directing my next words at all three of them. "Anyway, I wouldn't put it past Ravalos here to kill all of you after the shipment goes out, so he can have all the money for himself. That's probably why he *really* shot Rodriguez."

"She's lying!" Ravalos shouted. He strode back across the room and loomed over me threateningly with his gun. "Now shut up!" I obeyed him without another word. Believe me, nothing quells an appetite for argument like the sight of a gun barrel pointed straight at one's head. I felt a cold sweat break out all over my body as Ravalos' finger tightened on the trigger, but then he seemed to regain some semblance of control. "So, little girl." Ravalos smiled down at my white face, taking a sadistic pleasure in my fear. "Shall I shoot you here, where you will spoil my nice carpet with your blood?" He grinned and his good humor seemed to return as he gloated. "I will definitely kill you, but not right now. Not on the carpet, you see? And when I do, it will not be pleasant for you." He promised this matter-of-factly before turning back to his men.

Two of the men seemed not to have noticed my outburst at all and stared impassively at Ravalos. The third man, however, glanced at the door anxiously, as though he would have preferred to be on his way somewhere else. Ravalos noticed this and his eyes narrowed.

"What's the matter, Jorge?" Ravalos asked the third man softly. "You don't believe the lying little *gringa*, do you?"

"No, Señor Ravalos. I do not believe her." Jorge licked his lips and attempted a smile. "She is obviously lying." Despite his brave words, his gaze faltered. He looked away from Ravalos' eyes and down at the floor as he continued, "She did, however, raise an interesting point." The third man glanced across at his fellows as if for support and they stiffened, watching Ravalos as they studiously avoided Jorge's eyes.

"Yes?" Ravalos prompted softly, his smile fading rapidly. "And what would that be?"

"About the money." Jorge's smile was ingratiating. "Don't misunderstand me, Señor Ravalos, but you have said you will pay us. When will you pay us?" There was utter silence in the room and I saw a muscle jump in Ravalos' neck.

"I will pay you later the way I have always paid you,"

he murmured quietly. "And why does that matter right now, Jorge?" Jorge licked his lips again and an edge of fear came into his voice along with a slight whining note.

"I just thought that perhaps, today, because of this interference by the *gringa,* we could do things a little bit differently," he suggested, cautiously. "But of course, not if it inconveniences you, Señor Ravalos." These words were spoken with the utmost respect. But that's not how Ravalos took them.

"Perhaps you do not like the way I do things around here?" Ravalos continued, his tone rising slightly. The hapless Jorge shook his head mutely, looking at his partners for help. But there was none coming from that quarter. They stared impassively at Ravalos while Jorge cringed.

I wanted to warn Jorge that Gabriela, Velazquez and I had seen firsthand what Ravalos did to people who didn't like the way he ran things, for example Rodriguez, but something told me it might be unwise to attract Ravalos' attention just then.

Suddenly, oddly, Ravalos' mood seemed to change. He laughed heartily, throwing back his head in a fine display of white teeth and I felt him turn on his charm as if a powerful physical presence had just entered the room. Once again his face became handsome as he turned to Jorge, still cowering in front of him.

"I like an independent thinker." Ravalos' next words took everyone by surprise. "Perhaps I should promote you." Jorge stared at him, clearly at a loss. "I will promote you to Rodriguez' job," Ravalos told him, all teeth. "If he's dead, as you say, he would have wanted it that way. " Jorge grinned hesitantly as Ravalos enveloped all three of his men with his smile. The tension seemed to leave the room abruptly.

"Just look at us all!" Ravalos remarked cheerfully,

sliding the gun into the pocket of his jacket. "We stand here, fighting like chickens when there is work to be done." Ravalos reached out and clapped Jorge on the back, perhaps just a little too heartily, I thought.

Jorge staggered a little but looked at Ravalos with an uncertain smile as Ravalos turned to his men. "Go on now, quickly check if Rodriguez is alive, which I doubt. If he is dead, you two can finish the loading while Jorge and I take care of the mess here." Ravalos waved two of the men toward the door, putting up a hand to stop Jorge from joining the others. "Not you, Jorge. I will need you to help me here.

"*Sí, Señor,*" Jorge replied, now apparently eager to do Ravalos' bidding. When the sound of the other two men's footsteps had echoed away down the long tiled hallway leading to the garage, Ravalos turned his back on us all and walked away to stand before the picture windows, staring out of them thoughtfully.

"Maribel, my love, would you please go get my cell phone from the bedroom?" He turned and gave her a persuasive smile. She nodded and smiled back, all trace of anxiety lifting from her face in a flash.

"Of course, Antonio. Are we going away?" He nodded at her.

"Yes we are going away, just as soon as I finish up my business here."

"Good." She wrinkled her nose at the rest of us. "Because I don't think I like it here any more, Antonio." With these words she left the room, her slippers slapping on the tiled floor as she disappeared from sight down the hallway.

The newly promoted Jorge shifted his weight from foot to foot, seeming uncomfortable for a man who had just landed a career advancement, and I for one didn't blame him for being uneasy. I didn't trust Ravalos any more than he did.

Ravalos turned away from the windows finally, and fixed Jorge with his most dazzling smile. I felt the beauty of the man tug at me despite what I knew of his character and I couldn't help but be impressed by the sheer power of his charisma.

"Jorge, let us have a drink together, to toast our new arrangement." He added, "The others can finish the job and then you and I will take care of our little," here he gestured to where Gabriela, her father and I stood, "problems." He ended the sentence amiably, his eyes crinkling into a smile. What a creep! Jorge relaxed somewhat, seeming to heave a silent sigh of relief and I saw Ravalos glance at the Persian carpet under his feet.

"You will find a bottle of tequila in the kitchen, bring it here with two glasses and we will drink together," Ravalos suggested evenly and Jorge turned to obey him, still smiling. Two seconds later Ravalos went after him, very quietly.

There was a long moment of silence, then a gurgling thud and the sound of something heavy being dragged across the floor. Velazquez, Gabriela and I all stared at each other in horror as a door slammed in the kitchen then footsteps came hurrying along the hallway toward us. When Ravalos rejoined us, he was alone.

He closed the door behind him, turning toward us while scrubbing distastefully at his hands with a linen handkerchief. I couldn't help noticing that there was fresh blood on his white pants, near the cuff and I stared at him in horror, thinking of what had just happened to Jorge. Ravalos noticed my reaction and arched a dark brow at me in amusement.

"You killed Jorge," I breathed. Ravalos gave me a maniacal smile.

"Believe me, soon it will not matter to you," he told me with evident satisfaction. "I will kill you too."

CHAPTER FOURTEEN

Maybe so, but you'd better be careful," I told him, desperate now. "Señor Velazquez is right. There will be a lot more people asking questions around here pretty soon and when the three of us are found dead there will be even more questions," I retorted.

"Who says they will ever find you?" Ravalos' eyes narrowed in macabre amusement and I knew he had a plan already.

"Antonio? What's going on?" Maribel came tripping down the hall to join us, holding a small black cellphone in one perfectly manicured hand and a can of chilled coke in the other. Then she stared down at her feet with distaste and I followed her gaze.

Her fluffy pink slippers were stained with blood and as she took a few steps further into the room I noticed that she had left behind a trail of bloody slipper-prints. I felt a chill go down my spine as she carefully stepped out of the slippers and padded barefoot across the Persian carpet to hand the cell phone to Ravalos.

"I wanted a soda and there's blood in the kitchen," Maribel observed, "lots of it." Ravalos nodded and tucked the cell phone into the pocket of his slacks.

"One of the men cut himself on something sharp." He explained tersely.

"Oh," she said. A small frown appeared on her brow.

"He should have cleaned up his mess," she added peevishly. "Antonio, when are we leaving?"

Ravalos threw her an impatient glance and was opening his mouth to reply when from the direction of the garage came the sound of a disturbance. At first I thought that Ravalos' men had discovered Jorge's body and were raising the alarm but the noise seemd to come from farther away than that. Gabriela and I exchanged quick, hopeful glances.

There was a burst of what sounded like gunfire then more shouting. Ravalos whipped around, his face contorting like a mask as running feet approached the door to the room.

"¡Policía! Open up!" Someone shouted from outside. There was a pause as Ravalos reached for his gun, readying himself for an attack. Maribel's jaw dropped and she gazed at the door in stupefaction.

"Watch out!" I screamed, "he has a gun!" Ravalos turned and shot at me, his mouth working strangely as he pulled the trigger but he was in a hurry and missed. I hurled myself onto the floor, scrambling out of the line of fire behind the couch while Gabriela and her father also managed to take cover.

I watched cautiously from behind the couch as Ravalos pumped a few rounds of bullets into the door, apparently hoping to shoot his besiegers right through it. This resulted in silence on the other side of the door. Then I recognized Officer García's voice.

"Ravalos, we know you're in there. Put your gun down and come out." When Ravalos said nothing, Officer García continued. "Ravalos, we have taken your men into custody and your house is surrounded by the police. Look out the window, you can see them. Believe me, there is nowhere you can go."

In reply Ravalos fired several more rounds of bullets

through the door. There was silence again then a hail of answering fire and that splintering sound a door makes when it's shot to pieces. When the bullets finally stopped, Maribel stage-whispered across the room,

"Antonio, I think we should go now!" Ravalos ignored her and backed away from the door, looking wildly out of the windows as if to verify Officer García's words. What he saw was sufficient to bring a string of curses to his lips and I crouched behind the couch, trying to make myself as small as possible. Ravalos crossed the room and seized me by the hair, pulling me viciously to my feet.

"Ouch!" Desperately, I kicked him hard in the shins, hoping to make him let go of me but he only shifted his grasp from my hair to my arm which he twisted behind my back and up between my shoulder blades. With a splintering crash the double doors at the far side of the room slammed open and Officer García entered the room. Close behind him I saw Father.

"Don't move or I kill the girl," Ravalos warned them both and they froze. Officer García and Father exchanged worried glances, then they both lowered their guns very slowly. I was a little surprised that the police had given my father a weapon.

"Now." Ravalos spoke very deliberately. "You will let me go. No one will interfere with us as we leave the house, do you understand me?" I met Father's eyes in a silent plea for help as Officer García spoke.

"Ravalos, it will do you no good to try and run away. Your house is surrounded and your shipment has been impounded. There is no place you can hide." Ravalos stiffened and stroked my temple with the gun. The barrel felt very cold.

"It would be a shame if this one had to die, wouldn't it? Such a pretty face, so young." Ravalos' voice was almost silky as he continued in a completely weird matter-of-fact way, "Let me go and I let her go. Otherwise I kill her before your eyes." Nobody spoke and I saw Officer García signal to Father to start backing away from Ravalos.

"You can't trust him — he'll kill me anyway!" I told them both urgently. "He shoots his own men right in the back." Ravalos yanked my arm painfully and I felt something give there so I stopped talking, gasping in pain. Ravalos resumed his demand.

"You will instruct your men to let me leave in my car. Or I will kill her now."

"You are making a mistake, Ravalos," García told him tersely. "You cannot go far. Do not hurt the girl or I myself will see you go down."

I caught a glimpse of Gabriela's face, pale and terrified then, to my dismay, Officer García turned to gesture at the rest of the police force, some of them still crouching in the shadows of the hallway, and called out, "Move back!" Father's face was pale as he watched them file back down the hallway, making room for Ravalos and me to pass.

"Antonio, wait," Maribel called after him, sounding lost. "Wait for me!" Ravalos replied brusquely,

"You'll only slow me down."

He turned away from her and Maribel spoke again, plaintively, "But Antonio, I want to go with you."

"Shut up, you idiot." He was clearly nearing the breaking point. Maribel's eyes filled with tears and she stared at him uncomprehendingly, her lower lip trembling as she whispered,

"But Antonio..." He turned his back on her.

"Move it, you little brat," Ravalos muttered into my ear, ignoring Maribel's tears. "I will enjoy killing you when we are far from here." I paid his words no heed, watching for my chance to escape.

"He's going to kill me anyway," I told one motionless police officer, who then backed away warily and watched as we walked past. "Why don't you just shoot him now?"

Ravalos tapped me hard on the head with the barrel of his gun and growled, "They will not stop us because of this. Be quiet and do not forget that I can kill you whenever I want to." We had reached the garage, where several police cars were parked in a tight circle, surrounding Ravalos' men who all were wearing handcuffs and dismayed expressions.

As we watched, two of the police officers backed slowly away, making room for Ravalos to pass. He pushed me roughly toward the Mercedes parked near the fully loaded truck and when I sprawled across the side of the car he opened the front door and gave me a vicious shove inside.

I scrambled away from him and sat up, trying the door on the other side only to find it locked. I sure didn't want to be trapped in a car with Ravalos but I couldn't get out. Officer García and Father stood behind us helplessly, watching as Ravalos started the Mercedes.

"You'd better just stay quiet," he warned me, sparing me one sinister glare before turning his attention to the task of driving. I debated taking my chances anyway, gun or no gun and trying to clobber him or something while there were police officers around to help me. Before I could make my move Ravalos put the car into gear and floored it, heading down the open driveway.

I didn't imagine he'd go very far before stopping to kill me. I knew there was no way he would ever let me go free, even if he had promised to do so in exchange for his freedom. I tried the door handle again, pulling at it with all my strength but it was locked and Ravalos snapped at me,

"I told you to sit still! And attach your seat belt. I don't want you moving around."

"I *am* sitting still, you slime ball!" I snapped back at him. I knew I was a goner anyway so there seemed no point in hiding my dislike. Besides, he was too busy driving to smack me just then. Ravalos swung the car around in a wide arc as we passed the house and accelerated slightly as he headed for the road.

I was praying for a miracle when it occurred. We were moving pretty fast and when we reached the crest of the hill along which Ravalos' driveway ran I saw Father's rental car parked at an angle across the driveway, blocking it where it met the road. There were walls on either side of the driveway, and Ravalos had no option but to brake hard. We began to skid out of control. Then I saw an opportunity when Ravalos' gun slid from his lap in the confusion, falling to the left onto the floor of the car.

Cursing, he bent to retrieve the gun and I leaned toward him, grabbed the steering wheel and turned it sharply, stomping my foot as hard as I could on the corner of the brake pedal. It wasn't easy to reach, but I just got a piece of it. Ravalos' head hit the dashboard with a sharp crack and then he went limp, sliding back down to lie across the seat in a heap. For a moment I couldn't believe it was over. I felt sudden, intense relief over my narrow escape. Then I wanted to throw up.

"I guess you should have buckled up," I muttered shakily. Looking at his inert body I saw with some relief that he was still breathing. I mean, I disliked the man entirely but I didn't want to be responsible for his death.

After fumbling for a moment to remove my seat belt, I reached past him, found the master lock to release the door on my side and climbed out, shaking with relief. Someone ran toward me in the growing darkness and I recognized Rudy.

"K.C., are you all right?" He reached for me, as if

assuring himself that I was truly standing there and I gave him a shaky smile as he pulled me to him and hugged me, hard enough to take my breath away.

"I think so," I told him once he let me breathe again. Rudy turned to study Ravalos.

"Nice work, K.C..." he told me approvingly.

"Me?" I couldn't take all the credit. "I wouldn't have been able to do it if you hadn't distracted him. That was you who parked the car there, right?" Rudy smiled, his concerned expression replaced by one of self-conscious modesty.

"Well, yes," he admitted as Officer García came running to join us, closely followed by Father. Officer García was carrying a drawn gun but when he saw me and Rudy standing there and Ravalos inert on the seat of the car he lowered it slowly, an amazed expression crossing his face.

"Are you all right?" Officer García and Father asked simultaneously. Rudy and I smiled back at them. Despite my bruises I had never felt better. I found a tremendous sense of relief in the knowledge that Ravalos and his men would never be able to bother me again.

"I'm fine," I replied, knowing that it was true. I gestured at Ravalos' unmoving form. "But he sort of had an accident."

"How did it happen?" Officer García crossed to inspect the Mercedes and its inert passenger more intently.

"I sort of stomped on the brake and he wasn't wearing a seat belt," I admitted, watching him warily.

"Very well done, *Señorita*." Officer García gave me an approving grin over his shoulder. "He seems to be bruised but alive. We were lucky that none of us was hurt." Officer García finished his examination of Ravalos and waved for two of his men to approach. "Except for Salvador," he continued, exhaling heavily into his mustache, "but he'll be all right after a week or two." (I later learned that one of the police officers had taken a bullet in the arm during the initial roundup of Ravalos' men.)

We were joined by a half-dozen other officers from the house, having secured the premises, and soon we had a small crowd gathered around the Mercedes. Someone had called for an ambulance and it arrived while the police were taping off the scene of the accident. I watched, feeling curiously detached as the medics gingerly extricated Ravalos and put him on a stretcher. I couldn't help noticing how beautiful his face was, even(especially!) in unconsciousness.

The police escorted Father, Rudy and me back inside the house where they encouraged us to sit down after our ordeal. I was happy to comply. Two of García's officers were tending to Velazquez' wounds, first applying pressure to slow the flow of blood and then taping on bandages while two medics carefully lifted him onto on a stretcher. At our return Gabriela jumped to her feet and flew across the room to embrace me.

"K.C.!" she wept happily, "I never thought I'd see you again."

"Me too." I was equally moved. Across the room Maribel was sitting on a chair sobbing, her face streaked with tears. One of the officers put a gentle hand under her arm, lifting her to her feet and she allowed him to escort her quietly from the room to a waiting police car outside. That was the last I ever saw of Maribel.

I watched as two officers wheeled Jorge's shrouded body out of the kitchen on a gurney, pushing it silently down the hallway toward the garage. The blood stains on the sheet covering him were so vivid as to be surreal and I found myself having a serious nervous reaction. All the fear I'd pushed aside came flooding in and it was a long time before I could stop shaking.

"Thank you, K.C.," Señor Velazquez murmured up at me from the stretcher. "My daughter tells me it was you who freed her and saved our lives." I shot a quick glance at Gabriela who nodded and smiled at me.

"But we did it together," I reminded her. "I couldn't have done it alone." Rudy was standing very close to Gabriela, solicitously hovering over her and he nodded at my words.

"You were both really brave," he told us. "Facing down Ravalos like that..." He stopped speaking as Father turned to eye him thoughtfully.

"And how would you know about that? In fact, what are you doing here? I thought I told you to stay at the Velazquez' house until I returned," he said. Rudy swallowed, his eyes meeting mine for a split second as he replied steadily, "I took the car after you left and drove here by myself." This was my learner-permit-only brother speaking, the one who had been forbidden to drive unless strictly supervised.

"You did, did you?" Father rubbed a thoughtful hand along his jawline. "I see."

Rudy and I gave each other swift glances of reassurance and I put in loudly, "And I'm sure glad you did, Rudy. Otherwise Ravalos would have killed me when he left the driveway, I know he would have." The memory of my terror in being trapped in the Mercedes with Ravalos stopped me and I shook my head. "Thanks," I told Rudy again.

"You'd do the same for me," he told me steadily as Gabriela slipped her hand into his.

After the police had finished asking Velazquez, Gabriela and me for our initial statements and had finally left us alone, Father turned to fix me and Rudy with a weary stare. There was no doubt in my mind that he was glad for our safety, but at the same time I could tell that he was not a happy camper.

"Let me tell you two kids something. I am so incredibly

glad to see you safe." His eyes shimmered oddly and he continued, resolutely, "But you better believe me, we're going to talk about this in the morning." He shifted his gaze from me to Rudy. "The chances you kids take... And you, K.C." He fixed me with an accusing stare. "Didn't I tell you not to leave the hotel in the first place?"

"Yes," I muttered, and scuffed the ground with my shoe.

"I can see we really need to have a family meeting but here isn't the right time or place. We'll talk later." Rudy and I exchanged relieved glances and Father's eyes narrowed somewhat in amusement as he continued, "And that doesn't mean you two are off the hook either, you understand me?" We nodded back at him more soberly and he straightened up, seeming suddenly exhausted.

I noticed for the first time that Father had a sort of grey look about him, as though he had been scared half to death. Which he probably had. I felt a stab of genuine remorse for what I had put him through and said softly,

"I'm sorry Father, truly I am. But I had to do it." Father nodded resignedly at me, some of the lines in his face disappearing as he studied my face.

"I know you're sorry, K.C. I know you did what you thought was the right thing for the moment." He ruffled my hair gently then hugged me, almost as hard as Rudy had. "Don't worry kid, we'll work it all out later."

One of Officer García's men gave us a ride back to Puerto Vallarta but I couldn't tell you how the trip went. My last memory was of someone kind of escorting me up to my room and then I fell totally asleep, deeply and soundly.

CHAPTER FIFTEEN

The next morning after breakfast Father, Rudy and I visited Señor Velazquez in the local hospital, *Hospital Medasist*, where he was recovering from surgery to extricate the bullet Ravalos had lodged in his thigh. He seemed a little pale and tired but was in good spirits.

"*¡Ay, mis amigos!*" he exclaimed heartily, beckoning us into the room and Gabriela waved at me from across his bed.

"K.C.! How nice to see you." A good night's sleep had done wonders for my friend, she was once again the cheerful person I'd met on the beach.

"You too, Gabriela." We smiled at each other a little shyly. The last time I had seen Gabriela, she had been heading for home in the back seat of a police car.

"Hello. You must be Señor Flanagan. I am Angela Velazquez." The words were uttered by a small, plump lady with fine black eyes and a wide smile. She was sitting next to Gabriela at Velazquez' side, her fingers entwined with his on the coverlet of the bed. We introduced ourselves, shaking hands all around and I could easily see where Gabriela's good looks came from.

"Look!" Velazquez pointed to a folded newspaper on the nightstand beside him. "We are famous!" Gabriela handed the paper across and Father unfolded it as he took a chair on the other side of Velazquez' bed. Rudy and I perched on folding chairs near the door.

"Ravalos is being charged with three counts of murder and drug smuggling." Gabriela told us all with satisfaction as Father finished skimming the article and handed the paper to Rudy, who studied it and handed it to me. I saw a smiling head and shoulders shot of Ravalos adorning the front page but the article in Spanish accompanying it was too complex for me to read. "He will be in prison for the rest of his life," Gabriela concluded. I smiled a little.

"Good. No more than he deserves." I remembered Casteñada, Rodriguez, and Jorge. With the exception of Casteñada, who had been an innocent victim, they had been pretty mean but even so they hadn't deserved their fate at the hands of Ravalos. Not to mention the victims of his drug smuggling.

"What I don't get is how this all ties in to the law firm, *Sanchez y Sanchez,*" I admitted. "Were they smuggling drugs too?" Father heard my words and supplied the answer to my question.

"It turns out that Ravalos has been laundering the money he made from his smuggling with the help of the law firm. And he had a protector, the senior state prosecutor, a Señor Colón, who interfered with the police investigations in exchange for heavy bribes. Rodriguez was the middle man between Colón and Ravalos. In fact, you saw them together at Chico's Paradise. It is only because Rodriguez survived being shot by his boss that he was willing to talk, in exchange for a deal on sentencing for the murder of Casteñada. The police are searching for Colón right now but he has apparently fled Mexico. No one knows where he is."

"Laundering?" Gabriela put in, clearly unfamiliar with the term and Rudy explained.

"When someone takes money they can't account for

and puts it elsewhere where it looks normal, that's what we call 'laundering.' I mean, Ravalos couldn't really tell the world he made millions of dollars from drugs, could he? But he had to explain where it all came from just the same. So he gave money to the law firm instead. They probably just invested it for him, or something, so it would look like he made the money on something legitimate."

"Laundering. I see. Well, *Señor* Ravalos can do some real laundering from his new *residencia*, in a Mexican jail." Gabriela practiced the new word as she and Rudy grinned at each other, mutually appreciative. Apparently now that we were all out of danger, their flirtation was back on.

"You're pretty close, Rudy," Father nodded. "Actually, the law firm *Sanchez y Sanchez* was doing even more than that. I did some investigating after you told me about finding a link between Rodriguez and the law firm, K.C." I nodded as he continued. "*Sanchez y Sanchez* has been involved with Ravalos Construction quite a bit in the last few years."

"Oh, really?" I asked, my interest piqued. Father nodded.

"Yes. Ravalos and Sanchez apparently worked together to create several construction companies all over Mexico. And that's where Ravalos' money went."

"But there's nothing wrong with that," I protested. "Surely Ravalos could invest his money in a construction company if he wanted to." The others were staring at me with odd expressions on their faces so I clarified, "That is, he could if he were an ordinary person instead of an evil, drug smuggling murderer."

"You're absolutely right as far as that goes," Father nodded at me, "but there's more. You see, the companies don't actually exist. They only exist on paper. The construction companes were only a front."

"How can they not exist if Ravalos was putting his money into them?" Rudy asked, puzzled.

"They don't exist physically," Father told us. "I had someone check on three out of five of Ravalos' most recently formed companies and there's nothing there except empty offices where the corporate headquarters are listed." I thought about the deserted construction area I had found through an address in the phone book.

"So Ravalos was using the companies as a front to make it look like he was getting all his money through building stuff." I deduced.

"Which he was, in a way," Velazquez put in dryly from his bed. We all turned to look at him as he went on, "Ravalos has been building a smuggling empire on the coast for many years now, fooling the people of Bucerías into thinking his success was the result of his construction business. I knew him when he was a young boy. We went to school together." Velazquez' tone was oddly reminiscent and he smiled apologetically at us.

"He was always so good-looking, life came so easily to him." Velazquez' smile faded and he frowned. "But I didn't know he was smuggling drugs until just yesterday, when a friend of Casteñada told me Casteñada had tried to go to the police. That's why Ravalos and Rodriguez had to kill him."

"Was Casteñada one of the smugglers, too?" I wondered aloud. Velazquez shook his head.

"No. Just the opposite, he was an ordinary fisherman and that is what he wanted to remain. You see, Ravalos was greedy. He couldn't be content with what he had, he always wanted more. He began to expand his smuggling business along the coast and when the local fishermen objected, he either killed them or forced them to work for him." Velazquez had our full attention now.

"Señor Casteñada refused to work for Ravalos and also refused to keep quiet about what Ravalos was doing, so Ravalos had him murdered when he threatened to go to the police."

Gabriela finished her father's story. "That's where you came in, K.C."

"I see." I frowned, thoughtfully. "Does any of this have anything to do with the competing offer on the property, or was that just a coincidence?" Father nodded.

"It does, as a matter of fact. Ravalos was planning to buy the lot next door to Rodriguez' place and develop it himself, probably for smuggling, but maybe just to keep nosy *norteamericano* neighbors away." Father's face cleared a little. "But now that Ravalos is in jail the offer has been withdrawn. Even if Ravalos hadn't been caught, the things I found out about *Sanchez y Sanchez* pretty much put them out of the running for the property. The seller wants nothing to do with *Sanchez y Sanchez* anymore." Father gave me a wry smile. "I guess I owe you one for that, K.C."

"Thanks, K.C." Gabriela nodded warmly. "You saved us."

"Don't thank me," I protested her compliment sincerely, "I'm lucky to be alive. I see that now." I looked at Father apologetically. "I nearly got myself killed because I was so stupid." Father looked at me consideringly and his face softened.

"K.C., despite your mistakes you did a good thing. You helped your friend, or at least you intended to and luckily, things worked out. You also put a really bad guy behind bars for the rest of his life and that's a lot." I could hardly believe my ears, Father was actually praising me.

"But I disobeyed you," I reminded him, foolishly. He nodded.

"I know, and you'd better believe it will affect your privileges when we get home, but for now I've decided to let you both off the hook." He included Rudy in his glance. "That's right, Rudy, you too." My brother and I exchanged careful looks.

"I think I've learned my lesson," I told my Father fervently. "I'm never investigating another murder again." I really meant it but Rudy grinned at me.

"Not for another week at least! Right K.C.?"

"Oh, knock it off." I had to smile at his words in spite of myself. "This time I really mean it. No more detecting!" Father and Rudy simply laughed at me as Gabriela, her mother and her father looked on with indulgent smiles.

* * *

CHAPTER SIXTEEN
(EPILOGUE)

There's more to the story than that. I mean, we were all overnight heroes. The local newspapers interviewed Rudy, Gabriela and me, making us tell and re-tell the story of our exploits. The mayor of Bucerías even declared a *fiesta* in our honor and the whole town turned out to party with us at the ground-breaking ceremony for the new development.

Father was a happy man, the real estate deal had gone through just the way he'd wanted and construction would soon begin on the project he had been sent to facilitate. He spent the rest of his time in Puerto Vallarta planning for the future with the local coordinators for the development effort while Rudy and Gabriela and I hung out every day on the beach, mastering the art of using jet skis and swimming to our heart's content.

Rudy and Gabriela were good friends by the time we left Mexico but they never did become an item. I mean, they might have if we'd lived in Mexico but Gabriela lived too far away from us for Rudy to see her very often.

She did come to visit us in Montreal about a month later though, and stayed with us for almost two weeks. We had a great time showing her all around town, and Rudy took her white-water rafting through the Lachine Rapids on the mighty St. Lawrence River. I actually went along too, and it really was exciting, because as we were getting our float jackets on,

I saw to my amazement the heavy-set, toad-looking, — but that's another story. For another day. And it's a heck of a story, too.

It was hard to watch Gabriela get on the plane back to Mexico. She and I still keep in touch and I plan to look her up the next time I go to Mexico, (which might be next fall because I'm signed up for an extracurricular archeology class with a field trip to the Yucatan peninsula and its famous pyramids, including some beach time in Cancún). Well, I'll call her anyway. It's pretty far from one Mexican coast to the other.

All in all though, I would have to say that my time in Puerto Vallarta was time well spent. It may not have been the perfect vacation, and in fact looking back now I see that I was lucky to emerge relatively unscathed from my experiences. I do like to think that despite my mistakes I did the right thing for the most part, and I'm still glad that Ravalos got a life sentence, and Rodriguez not much less. I hear that Mexican jails don't come equipped with poolside cabanas and cocktails at Happy Hour. But they do have a very large *laundry*.

Anyway, the excitement helped me to keep a journal about what happened to me on my trip and I hope you enjoyed hearing all about it. Thanks for tuning in! Let me know if you ever want to see the pictures of Puerto Vallarta and Bucerías. I posted them up on the web, and of course I have e-mail.

Just connect to http://www.rdppub.com/KookCase.

¡See ya!
K.C. Flanagan

Here is an excerpt from the second novel in the
K.C. Flanagan, girl detective™ series,
CHAOS IN CANCÚN.

I crept closer to the edge of the cliff, reaching for my binoculars and peering down in fascination. What appeared to be an orange buoy bobbed violently atop the waves below me, a marker for what I couldn't imagine.

"Careful," Julian said, as he grabbed my arm and pulled me gently back from the edge of the cliff. "The wind can be pretty strong at this height. You don't want it to take you by surprise up here." His blue eyes were friendly and frank.

"I saw something down there," I told him as he released my arm.

"Oh?" he said, his dark brows arching upward in surprise. "What?" I shook my head, frowning.

"I couldn't quite make it out, but there seemed to be an orange buoy down there, by the cliffs."

"That's not possible," he told me gently. "Those rocks are off limits, they're far too dangerous for people to approach and no reason for a buoy. It must have been a piece of flotsam." Rudy had strolled over to join us in time to catch Julian's remark.

"Seeing things again, Kook Case?" he asked me, offering a commiserating smile to Julian. "Don't mind my little sister, Julian. She's got an over-active imagination."

"I do not!" I protested.

"We all have our little idiosyncrasies," Julian commented obliquely and, giving me a crooked sideways smile took my arm gently once more, steering me further away from the edge of the cliff. I thought that my little spat with Rudy had gone unnoticed, but then I saw Linda eyeing both of us thoughtfully.

"How about if Rudy and your father drive back to the hotel in one cart and you and Julian and I take the other cart? I'd love to hear about your day, honey," Linda suggested. Julian and I exchanged friendly glances.

"It's all right with me," I agreed.

"No problem," Julian said, and handed her the keys to the cart. "Is it all right if you drive, Linda? I have a few notes to make on our progress today."

"Oh, but I might want to take pictures or write things down," Linda replied, holding the keys out to me. "How about you. K.C., you up for driving?"

"Sure," I smiled, happily accepting the keys.

Julian took the passenger seat and Linda sat behind me as I started the cart. The little engine sputtered to life, noisy but not noisy enough to prohibit conversation.

Julian pulled a small black notebook out of his shirt pocket and jotted something in it as I guided the cart along the road back to Isla Mujeres, following Rudy and Father. After he finished writing he turned to Linda and me with a smile.

"So, how do you like Isla Mujeres?"

"It's paradise," I told him quite sincerely, "glorious and quiet." In fact, the island was about as relaxed a place as anywhere I'd ever been.

Not that I was complaining, mind you. My last 'vacation' with Rudy and Father several months ago in Puerto Vallarta had turned into a "bang-bang" adventure as I'd tangled with a nasty drug smuggler. As far as I was concerned, peace and quiet were far preferable to that kind of action any day.

"Not much happens here," Julian shrugged. "It's not a big center of commerce or anything. The main industries here are tourism and fishing."

I nodded. The small town of Isla Mujeres was popular as a jumping-off point for tourists heading out to Cancún, Cozumel and Chichén Itzá.

"What does Isla Mujeres mean, anyway?" I asked Julian curiously.

"It means Isle of Women," he told me, "the Spanish conquistadors named it when they first came to the Yucatán Peninsula in 1517."

"Why? People say it's because this is where the Spanish buccaneers used to keep their women, um —" she stopped in mid-sentence, and out of the corner of my eye I saw her glance at me.

"Mistresses?" I supplied the missing word and Linda shrugged, then nodded.

"Well, captives, prisoners of war, ladies, you know," she finished somewhat lamely, obviously deeming a more colorful description to be unsuitable for one of my tender years.

"Spanish buccaneers huh?" I repeated. "You mean, as in pirates?"

There was a short pause and then Julian answered me.

"This island is famous for having once been a stopping point for

Spanish slave traders and pirates, yes."

"The entire Yucatán coast was frequented by merchants and pirates in the mid 1500's, wasn't it?" Linda asked and Julian nodded in response. I concentrated on driving while Julian and Linda talked about the history of the Spanish invasion of Mexico.

In 1517 Francisco Hernandez de Cordova was the first official Spaniard to see the 'New World,' as South America was considered by Europeans. His discovery was followed by increasing interest from Spain, which in 1519 sent Hernan Cortès to buy Mayan slaves.

Eight years after that Francisco Montejo and his son had traveled inland, taking the Yucatán by force.

The Spanish conquest of the Mayan people was aided by the diseases the Spaniards had brought with them. Huge numbers of the Mayan people were believed to have been wiped out by smallpox, chicken pox and influenza, making the conquest a simple matter of medical fact.

"Like the black plague," Linda commented, taking notes as Julian went on.

"About that devastating to the Mayan population, yes," Julian confirmed.

We were more than halfway back to the town of Isla Mujeres and were passing what looked like a private airstrip on our right side. I wanted to study it along with the fairly posh neighborhood surrounding it more closely, but traffic was picking up now so I stayed alert.

"What were the Mayas like?" I asked, "before the Spanish came, I mean." I'd done a little reading on the subject myself but was still interested in hearing his opinion.

"Have you been to see any of the nearby Mayan ruins yet?" he answered my question with one of his own and I shook my head.

"No, why?"

"It would be easier to explain them if you had." He looked over his shoulder at Linda and asked, "Why don't we all go see Chichén Itzá together tomorrow? Are you free?" Linda's face lit up.

"Really?" She was obviously trying not to gush. "That would be great, Julian. I'll have to talk to James about it but as far as this article is concerned it would be best if I could interview you right at the location of your discovery."

"Discovery?" I repeated curiously. Linda leaned forward to explain:

"Julian was restoring part of the ancient city of Chichén Itzá and he discovered a stone calendar indicating the beginning of Mayan time. It is one of the most significant archaeological discoveries in recent years, K.C."

"Wow," I said, deeply impressed. Julian shot me a bemused glance. "One of the calendars used by the ancient Mayas is called the long count and dates back to 3114 B.C.," Julian explained. "We don't know why they chose that date, but it was very significant to them for some reason."

We were approaching the outskirts of the town of Isla Mujeres and driving required all of my concentration so I stopped talking. I was sharing the road with a chaotic jumble of pedestrians, sunburned tourists in swimsuits, mopeds, taxis and other golf carts.

If we had been somewhere else in the world, in Florida for example, the chaos would have been annoying, but this was Isla Mujeres; here it was cool, people were relaxed and in no particular hurry. Instead of the impatience which is common in congested areas there were smiles as each one waited courteously for the other to pass or turn in a display of civility too often absent from Norh American city driving.

I turned right at Matamoros and drove three blocks to the hotel Vista Del Mar. It was an easy building to spot from a distance, owing mostly to the fact that it was painted a deep aqua color, with dusky pink and purple balconies wrapped around the open front of the building.

Many of the buildings on Isla Mujeres were ultra-colorful and had brightly patterned awnings which served to shade the narrow sidewalks below and the pedestrians there. Still, a lot of people strolled along right in the middle of the street, making it a real challenge for me to maneuver the golf cart safely among them.

When we reached the hotel I turned into the small courtyard in back and parked there. Luiz, the man at the reception desk, took the keys from me with a smile. Father and Rudy were already inside the hotel, waiting for us in the lobby.

"Meet for dinner later?" Julian directed the question at Linda and after a quick glance at my father who nodded, Linda replied:

"Sure, the buffet is at eight." Julian nodded, collected his mail and headed upstairs to the apartment he and the other members of his crew were sharing.

"Well," Father said as we took the stairs up to our own apartment. "What do you think?"

"It's hot," Rudy replied fervently, fanning himself with a magazine.

"He's nice," Linda replied.

"About what?" I asked. Father led us down a long, mauve hallway with a pink tiled floor toward a narrow stairway arching up.

"About Isla Mujeres," Father clarified, unlocking the door which led to our apartment. We were staying for a whole week and so, instead of renting single rooms, Father and Linda had decided to take advantage of the fact that the Hotel Vista Del Mar also offered spacious family apartments for short term rent.

"The island is cool," I answered, following Rudy inside the foyer. The living room was quite large, and very colorful. The walls were pale aqua, the floor was tiled in deep blue-green, and most of the wooden furniture had been painted in black enamel. The instant he'd seen it Rudy had developed a fixation about the centerpiece of the room, a puffy purple sofa embroidered with a flamboyant red floral pattern.

"So, was Julian how you expected him to be?" Father asked Linda with curiousity as she tossed her straw hat on the hat stand and headed for the kitchen. Rudy sat gingerly on the sofa, eyeing it briefly as though uncertain if it were friend or foe, then switched on the TV.

"Not really," Linda replied from the kitchen, where she got a bottle of iced tea from the refrigerator, "although I guess I'd expected him to be a little more stuffy than he is. Anyone else want some tea?"

"Me," I answered quickly. The tropical sun made me thirsty.

"I'd like one," Father added.

"Me too," Rudy spoke up and Linda returned a moment later, bearing chilled bottles of iced tea which she handed around.

I waited until everyone had had a minute to sip their tea, then announced: "Julian had a great idea for tomorrow."

Father quirked an eyebrow at me. "What's that?"

"It's about Chichén Itzá," Linda explained. "He suggested that we go to the ruins tomorrow, and offered to give us a tour of the site."

"Sounds like a good idea. What do you think, Rudy?" Father asked, raising an eyebrow in his best Irish manner.

"Fine with me," Rudy answered.

"Let's do it then," Father said. Linda's grin lit up the room.

"Oh, James," she went to give him a big hug, burying her face in his chest, "you're such a doll." He gave her a tender smile and they kissed, right in front of us! It can be a little disconcerting the way they carry on like that, I mean, they've been dating for two years but they still act like smitten teenagers.

Rudy and I never really talked about it but I think we both assume they will get married someday, although they don't seem to be in any big hurry to formally tie the knot. Linda has her own apartment in Montreal, where she lives when she's not traveling on business and Father enjoys his independence too. For now, they seem pretty happy with the way things are.

Tactfully, Rudy and I strolled out and up onto the paved rooftop of the hotel, an open expanse which stretched along one side of our apartment like a private garden. There was a fountain up there, three large potted palms and several wicker chairs in a cluster near a round wooden picnic table.

Rudy and I stood there in silence, watching as the sun set over the sea, the blue-green sky deepening into midnight blue over the velvet water which washed in gentle waves onto the white sand. Five little boys were playing soccer in a circle on the beach, kicking the ball back and forth and laughing when the ball rolled close to the waves.

"I wonder what she's doing right now," Rudy murmured, his eyes on the soccer game, his thoughts obviously elsewhere.

"Pamela," I said with resignation. It was the only word which could get through to Rudy.

"She's great, isn't she." He said it with such conviction that I knew contradicting him would only result in serious discord. I just nodded, sinking into one of the wicker chairs, and as if on cue, Rudy took the chair opposite me and leaned forward with an earnest look.

"What if she meets someone else while I'm here?" he asked, and I shook my head gently, trying hard not to be impatient with him. I would have been more sympathetic toward Rudy, but this had been going on for a month and it was getting a little stale.

"Then she isn't right for you," I replied simply. Rudy's worried look increased slightly so I pointed out reasonably, "Look, Rudy, we'll only be here for a week. Then we'll head home and everything will be fine." His face brightened then sank.

"A lot can happen in a week," he sighed heavily, his shoulders slumping. Patiently, I decided to try another approach.

"Look, Rudy, you're a cool guy, what girl could possibly forget you in one week?" A small smile crossed his face.

"That's true," he admitted self-consciously. The sound of laughter drew our attention back to the room where Father and Linda were seated side by side on the sofa, laughing together at something she had just said.

"They're so happy," Rudy's wistful look returned. "I wish Pamela were here now."

"Well she's not, so snap out of it, all right?" My small reserve of sibling understanding was gone and Rudy turned a look of hurt surprise on me at my harsh words. I sighed, "I'm sorry Rudy, it's just that you've been going on and on about Pamela for weeks now and —." Rudy held up a hand, deeply injured.

"Never mind K.C. I can see you're just too young to understand." He left me with pained dignity, heading for his own room, and I watched him go with mingled pity and frustration.

It wasn't like Rudy to mope, but he was definitely moping. I was starting to feel a little worried about him but I really couldn't think of anything to do to help him snap out of it. And after his response to my latest advice I had to admit that tough love wasn't the best way to go.

I got up and wandered downstairs, strolling one block toward the deserted end of the north beach. For a while I stood and watched the waves roll in and then I noticed a large white yacht docked at one of two long concrete piers stretching out from shore. I contemplated it curiously.

I was pretty sure the yacht hadn't been there earlier in the day, I knew I would have remembered seeing it if it had been. I studied the big vessel closely, she was about seventy-five feet long, enameled white with gold trim. There might have been the gleam of a satellite dish on the top deck. I walked closer, intrigued.

A movement caught my eye and as I watched, a short, husky man in a white suit and panama hat strode into view. He paced across the deck to stand at the side of the railing, looking expectantly toward shore as though waiting for someone. He didn't notice me standing there, but something about him made me feel uneasy. Without even knowing why I shivered as I watched him turn away abruptly, his attention caught by a second man I now saw walking down the length of the pier to board the yacht.

The first man, the one in white, now had his back to me as he stood on deck talking to the newcomer who was wearing faded blue jeans and a nondescript soiled white work shirt. I could see his face and studied it closely.

He looked like he was about thirty-five years old or so, with thick blond hair cut stylishly short and a handsome, rugged face. As I watched, the man in white reached into his breast pocket and pulled out a fat manila envelope. I caught the glint of gold on an unusual pinky ring the man in white was wearing and frowned, wondering where I had seen that ring before. I took another step toward the pier, watching as the second man took the envelope and lifted the flap. He peered inside with a twisted smile, then glanced around furtively and stuffed the envelope hastily into the pocket of his pants. He left quickly without any goodbyes, hurrying back the way he'd come. The man in white turned to watch his progress, looking straight at me, and I gasped as he turned enough for me to get a clear look at his face.

It was a face I recognized from my recent experiences on the other side of Mexico, in the Pacific coast resort town of Puerto Vallarta, and although I had only seen its owner briefly, it was a face I would never forget. The man was Señor Hernan Colón, a notoriously corrupt member of the Mexican government who had been indicted on charges of protecting a ring of drug smugglers in Puerto Vallarta. He had fled Mexico for Ireland and then to Canada after his nefarious activities had been uncovered, but was extradited back to Mexico to face charges after I recognized him in Montreal.

Since I was one of the people who had been instrumental in bringing him to justice, you can imagine the shock of fear I felt at seeing him here on Isla Mujeres, when he was supposed to be in jail pending trial.

For a split second we stared at each other, mutual recognition crackling between us like a current of electricity, then Señor Colón shouted something unintelligible and pointed at me, his face contorting with rage as yet another man appeared from the inside of the yacht's cabin.

I watched in horror as the third man listened to Colón's shouted instructions then turned and sprinted toward the pier, heading in my direction. It was clear he was coming for me and although I had no way of knowing what his intentions were I had a definite feeling that he didn't mean to engage me in a simple chat about the weather.

I took off, running as fast as I could toward the concrete promenade ahead of me through thick white sand which slowed me despite my best efforts at speed. After about fifty yards I glanced over my shoulder, hoping that I had lost my pursuer, but he was hot on my trail, in fact he was gaining on me.

Sheer terror lent wings to my feet and when I reached the concrete promenade I sprinted through the small crowd of people gathered there to view the sunset, ignoring their stares as I headed for the safety of the jumble of houses about one hundred yards away.

From the commotion behind me it was evident that I was still being pursued so I didn't waste time looking over my shoulder but turned down a small side street, weaving in and out of the vendors' stalls, past rows of colorful hand-painted masks and ceramics. At some other time I might have paused to admire the art but I could hear the slap of my pursuer's feet on the cobblestones as he came after me through the crowd.

Despite the safety my hotel represented, I knew it would be foolish for me to head straight back there, since the last thing I wanted was for Señor Colón to know where I was staying (We were registered at the hotel under Linda's name, so Colón wouldn't be able to trace me directly).

I turned two corners in rapid succession and darted into the secluded courtyard of a private residence where I crouched behind a potted palm, watching for the seconds it took my pursuer to sprint past my hiding place and disappear down the street.

After I was sure he was gone I stood up shakily and looked around at the stupefied stares of an elderly couple who had evidently been sitting down to dinner in the quiet privacy of their own home before being rudely interrupted by my intrusion.

"Um, *lo siento, señora, señor,*" I shrugged and spread my hands, indicating that it had all been a mistake and that I was sorry to have disturbed them. "I'm sorry, please forgive me." The elderly man at the table exchanged puzzled glances with his wife who turned to me with a cool shrug, motioning away the impolite *gringa*. "I'll just be on my way now," I added apologetically, skulking back into the street.

I walked quickly back to the hotel Vista Del Mar, peering around myself every few steps for fear that I might again encounter Colón's henchman. The scariest part of the whole thing was wondering what Señor Colón was doing on Isla Mujeres in the first place, when he was supposed to be safely locked up in Mexico City.

That he had recognized me as I had recognized him was undeniable and it seemed clear from his reaction that he was not at all happy with my presence on the island. Dejectedly, I turned into the stairs leading to the veranda of the hotel, casting one last look over my shoulder to be certain I was unobserved before heading upstairs to tell Father what I had seen. I found him on the roof, looking for me.

If you don't live near a bookstore, you can order K.C. Flanagan books from the publisher by mail or fax, (using the following order form, and paying by check or Visa/Mastercard), or from the K.C. Flanagan Internet site on the World-Wide Web at http://www.rdppub.com/KookCase, (credit cards only).

Please mail to
Robert Davies Multimedia Publishing Inc.,
330-4999 St. Catherine St.,
Westmount, Quebec, Canada H3Z 1T3
or Fax to 514-481-9973

PLEASE SEND ME:

QTY	TITLE	PRICE	POSTAGE	TOTAL
	PANIC IN PUERTO VALLARTA	$9.99 CAN $6.99 US	$2	
	CHAOS IN CANCÚN	$9.99 CAN $6.99 US	$2	
			GRAND TOTAL	

NAME

ADDRESS

CITY–PROV./STATE

POSTAL CODE/COUNTRY

CHECK INCLUDED FOR $_____   OR

VISA/MASTERCARD #   EXP.